Dr. Sarcophagus and his
CARNIVAL OF
DARK DESIRES

Collected by
Mitchell J. Hyman

Edited by
Jeffrey M. Stundel

Cover and interior art by
Richard C. Livingston

This collection is dedicated to all who love the unusual and unique...

...and especially to those with the courage to publicly admit that they do.

Thank you, ladies and gentlemen – with apologies to any who may not quite fit into either category – for your coins and your consideration.

And now, without further ado, let the show begin.

SHOW GUIDE

MEET DR. SARCOPHAGUS

Can you feel them? All around you are watchful eyes. Are they looking at you? Or are they, like your own, seeking something that has no name? As your eyes adjust to the light from torches, fire barrels and the incandescent glow of familiar electric lights, you see the others. The other eyes that belong to just regular humans. That's all there is around you for now. There are no monsters in *my* darkness. Well, no monsters that weren't there already and brought in by the others like you. They, again, like you, bring only what your psyche can contain. I do not deal in monsters. I trade in something much more awesome and appetizing. But you'll see more of that very soon – for the moment, the people moving around you are the show.

Between the brightly colored, pinstriped tents and the garish banners advertising the thrills and delights of my show, you can see these people of whom I speak. What they see and hear makes their hearts race. I want to drink the cool sweat that beads on their brows. It is the liquor of fear and anticipation. Would that I could grab their heads and lap up that which is to me an intoxicating nectar, pooling sweet and honey-like in the creases. The stinging, pungent scent of dampened armpits is a perfume I cannot resist. It is my myrrh and frankincense, the smell of dark desires. And they bring it to me, their savior.

Yet I am no immaculate godling. I am merely who I am: one who is not a god, but who has been witness to the gods and goddesses, the arcane and mundane. I know how much the lines between them blur – and I know where those well rubbed edges of confluence meet, where the worlds of the seen and unseen mistakenly, yet unmistakably, blend like daubs of wet paint on a canvas. If you know where to look, you can see where blue and red make purple – and, more deliciously, where white and black make all the shades of gray that lead you, my guests, and this, my ever-growing family, here, to my carnival.

Ah, but that reminds me. I am being rude. I tell you that I know all about you and yet forget to properly introduce myself. I sometimes forget how much I remember, and with that my manners. I am Dr. Sarcophagus: and this is my Carnival of Dark Desires. What brought you hither? Does it matter?

Does it make you uncomfortable when I say that I know but you choose not to? Regardless, here is my promise – and I never lie. Truth is more satisfying – and often more entertaining – than fiction. I promise that you will not leave here disappointed. Changed? A bit worse – or better – for the experience? Well, that is another story.

As you pass from tent to tent, you will meet and be met and greeted by the members of my family of whom I spoke. I encourage you to enjoy and explore, to be amused and to be horrified; but please do remember to be respectful – they are my family. To most, they are called "freaks" – created either by nature or by choice. To me, well, I am the only father they have ever known – the carnival, their mother. Once, societies considered them a source of pride and honor – now, society is "enlightened" and paradoxically wishes them taken out of the light. It seeks to bury them in the darkness, along with everything else it wishes to deny about itself that it finds unpleasant. The light? It is blinded into self-deluding forgetfulness. But the darkness – the darkness remembers.

And waits.

Again, trust me when I say that you have nothing to fear from the shadows of my tents – they are nothing compared to the ones you cast.

But I am being overly melodramatic. Forgive me my weak attempts at showmanship and allow me to welcome you to my carnival, the last horse-drawn wagon show of its kind. As the world you left outside reckons time, it is the year…well, temporal concerns are of no matter to us. You are in a timeless world, and I encourage you to make the most of it. As each of you is aware, there are many things for which you must someday pay, but consider this my gift to you: free of charge.

Ah, but I hear the music coming up on our first act, and I know it is one you will not want to miss. You will see me from time to time throughout the evening – the carnival has dark desires of its own to which I must attend.

As do you.

And now, enjoy the show…

TENT 1

RAGGEDY DAN
Jeffrey Stundel (from a concept by Tori Fernandez)

Backstage, he creeps into a box that looks like a present. The box only comes up to his knees and is just wide enough to accommodate his broad shoulders. By degrees, he folds himself…smaller…smaller…his real father is to thank. The assistants quickly throw the lid on top of the box and rush it on stage just as Dr. Sarcophagus begins his introduction.

"Now, ladies and gentlemen, here to amaze and confuse the way you look at dolls is Raggedy Dan!"

The crowd is silent, only seeing a box under a spotlight. The act comes after a tattooed fire breather named Dragon, so who knows what will be next? The assistants flip open the front lid and step back.

The audience sees a motionless figure. They can see – are those stitches? – an arm…what looks like a foot…the top of a head? Like a spider crawling out of a matchbox, the form begins a slow extrication from its tiny prison. A scream from the audience breaks the silence – not a shriek of enjoyment. He likes the sound, but can't smile. It is part of the act.

Yes. The figure in the box is alive. An arm. A leg. Now more screams and gasps. A head soon follows, exposing wildly tousled, dirty blonde hair. Skin, slightly tanned, a roadmap of scars – some ugly and red, others pink and fading, some just white lines. In his ear, a fishhook instead of an earring – and his mouth. That mouth! It looks like a rag doll's, crosshatched. How did he eat – or talk?

With the spotlight on him, Raggedy Dan continues his act.

One assistant pulls the box to the edge of the stage while the other brings forward a chair. Raggedy Dan bends frighteningly forward like a creature with no spine, and then crazily twirls his upper body in a circle. Gasps and chokes erupt as he thrusts backward, bending at the waist, until his head is touching his calves. He is staring backwards, but he can still hear the sound of a patron vomiting and stifles a laugh. Pulling his body back to its erect self, he stumbles over to the chair and flops into it, lolling as if boneless.

1

The assistants drag five people from the audience to come up and see that Raggedy Dan is not faked – that he is a sewn up and pieced together person.

The first is a young couple in their early twenties. Raggedy Dan keeps his head down, staying as limp as a doll. The young man is a brave soul – when told that he can touch Raggedy Dan he quickly jumps at it. With slightly shaking hands, he reaches forward and strokes one of Raggedy Dan's arms. Raggedy Dan springs to life and looks up with a crazy glint in his eyes and a smirk on his face. This is what he loved: making others uncomfortable around him, to see them squirm made him happy. The young man gasps and steps back a few steps. His wife just looks and covers her mouth and begins to cry. They are escorted off the stage while the next three people come forward. And so the act proceeds.

Soon it is time for the climax. An assistant removes the chair, as Raggedy Dan begins twisting his limbs around his body like a pretzel. He wraps his arms through his legs and his legs above his head. He twists all around the stage for about seven minutes before it is time for him to get back into his wooden prison. As Raggedy Dan retreats into his box, like a hermit crab drawing itself into its shell, a smattering of confused applause is heard.

It is always so.

He is pushed offstage by the assistants, while Dr. Sarcophagus announces the next act, Bessie, the largest woman in the world. Once past the curtains, the assistants lift the lid. This time, Raggedy Dan – now just Daniel – extricates himself more quickly and less dramatically from his confines. "Nice job out there tonight. You really know how to freak out the audience members," says Gregory, one of the assistants. "Thanks," Daniel responds, somewhat sullenly, "but you say that every show – it gets boring." Wearily waving his arm about him he added, "As does all of this."

The other assistant, a pretty woman named Sarah Jean, tsks, "Now, Daniel. You should be happy. You have a great gig here. You have food, a place to sleep and, unlike some others here, a bit of cash to spend." Sarah Jean is Gregory's wife. They have been his second parents since they found him two years ago. When he was "raggedy" Daniel.

Gregory found him by a stream. Gregory's chores were simple: find fresh water; collect said water; bring the performers who couldn't get there on their own to said water and help them bathe. Sarah Jean was back at the carnival doing her seamstress duties.

The sun was slowly on a downward path and Gregory wanted to complete his task and get back to the carnival before night fell. He had an outdoorsman's innate sense of direction and "feel" for nature, so it wasn't too long before he found what he was looking for. He got down on his haunches and tasted the water — it was clean. Perfect, he thought. Now I can get back. But something stopped him as he got up.

It was a cough.

Not a cough to get his attention; just a general cough. Without making another move or a sound of his own, Gregory looked around and saw a small figure lying on a rock: a boy. He was close enough that he could see the boy's terrible leanness and tattered clothes; but he reminded himself that finding additional mouths to feed wasn't on his to-do list. So, silently, he slipped away back to the carnival.

When he told Sarah Jean, she was shocked that he simply left the boy there. "How could you do that? It wasn't too long ago that we were in trouble and someone was kind enough to take us in." Gregory opened and closed his mouth like a fish. He knew there was little use in arguing with her when she hooked onto a cause.

For Sarah Jean, the idea of a "boy" reminded her of how much she wanted to have a child — and their recent failure. She turned to Gregory and said, "You will take us both there, now, and help me bring that boy back here." Gregory had to demur. "But what about the rules of the carnival? We can't just bring him back here without —"

"We will bring him to see Dr. Sarcophagus once he's cleaned up," Sarah Jean said sternly. Gregory sighed and motioned for her to lead the way out the door.

The boy was still where Gregory found him. Gregory motioned for caution, but Sarah Jean was in no mind to listen. She simply marched up to the boy — Gregory was terrified. What if the kid was sick or violent? The words were out of his mouth before he realized it. "Sarah Jean — NO!"

Too late; but it didn't matter. The boy jumped up and backed away from her, more shocked than aggressive. "Stay away!" he yelled. "This is MY stream! You can't take it away from me!" In the lengthening shadows, Sarah Jean wasn't sure if it was a trick of the light coming through the tree branches; but the boy's skin seemed to be covered in...stripes? And what was that hanging from his ear that glinted so? She inched closer and saw that they weren't stripes — they were cuts and scars running wildly across his entire body.

"Please, let us help you!" she pleaded. "You're hurt!"

"I don't need any help!" was the shouted response. "I need these hurts — and no one can help me. Or be trusted! No one!"

Sarah Jean realized that the boy must have been abused by his parents — or by others. She had to proceed carefully. "Would it be okay if I just sat here for a while? It was a long walk here," she said without sitting down. She wanted him to give his approval — to be the one in charge. He warily eyed her. "Okay," he said suspiciously, "but only for a minute."

Gregory said nothing. He watched in the wings ready to leap in if the boy made a move towards her.

"Thank you…?" she said, allowing her voice to trail off in a probing question for his name. The boy bit. "Daniel. My name's Daniel."

"Daniel. My name is Sarah Jean. That man over there is my husband, Gregory." The boy hadn't moved. She spoke in even, matter-of-fact tones. "We live with a carnival. We're here to get water for the people. We've traveled far and we're all very thirsty." She stood up, stretched, and said, "But, if this is your stream, we'll leave it to you. Thank you, Daniel. I think I'm ready to go back, Gregory." She turned and walked towards her husband and was unsurprised – and smiled – to hear a voice say, "Wait. Did you say a 'carnival'?"

"Yes, Daniel," she said, stopping and returning to look at him, "a carnival. Would you like to see it?"

Carnival. She knew the word would melt like cotton candy in his mouth. He took a few hesitant steps towards her and said, "I'll follow you." It was then that Sarah Jean saw the fishhooks – and his face. Accustomed as she was to the carnival's residents, she was able to stifle an outward reaction. In his ears were large crescents of metal. There were others in his arms. And his face. She now understood why he kept smiling.

His feet were bare and covered in muck. Scars and freshly sewn cuts were scattered wherever his skin was visible. *I wonder how many scars he really has,* Sarah Jean thought. *They're probably deeper than they appear.*

Daniel got the first scar that mattered the day his father received his deepest cut. Robert Lee was an angry man and a mid-level executive at a New York bank. He had worked his way up from a humble clerk and proud of his achievement – not bad for a poor farmer's son from North Carolina.

Robert answered the door and accepted a telegram. He opened the envelope and, as quickly as he opened it, Daniel, his mother and sister could hear violently crumpling paper and muffled oaths all the way in the kitchen.

"What is that, Robert?" His mother asked in a whispered voice. Daniel and his sister, Samantha, peered around her. "Get out of here – go to your rooms. NOW!" he bellowed. Soothingly, their mother ordered, "Go. We'll finish our game later."

When the children had departed, Robert hurled the ball of paper at his wife's face. "What is it, Lillian? It's my notice – that's what it is!" Doubly stunned, Lillian Lee slowly bent over and picked up the paper. As she was un-crumpling it, he snatched it out of her hands. "No," she said, her voice quivering in both fear of both her husband's loss and her husband, "You've been with them for over twenty years. You just made manager – you were in charge!"

"Really, you dumb sow? Really? Well, let me read something to you. 'Robert Lee. We are no longer in need of your position at our bank. We regret that we will be losing such a great asset. Arrangements will be made to return your personal effects. Sincerely, Gram Claric.' 'In charge?' He fired me with a piece of paper!" He shook the paper under her nose and hurled it to the floor.

Daniel, unseen while watching from the landing, coughed.

His father whirled at the noise and stared at him, red faced. He shuddered and then exploded, "I can't trust anyone, can I?!" He spun a wild backhand at his wife, who reached for him as he stormed to the stairs. As she fell to the floor he bounded up, taking off his belt. "No! No one! Not even my own flesh and blood! Well, we'll see about that!" Daniel only got one step higher when he felt his father's meaty hand in the collar of his shirt, pulling him backwards. The last thing he remembered was the elder Lee's wild eyes and a belt buckle coming down as his father shouted, "I won't be anyone's puppet! I'm in charge here! I pull the strings!"

When he came to, Samantha was holding a cold compress on his face as his mother was saying, "...just a few more." He felt a throbbing and a repeated pulling above his eyebrow. He instinctively flinched away from the pain. "Shh...no, love," his mother said, "stay still so Mommy can sew her little doll back together again." Lillian Lee was an expert seamstress and, as such, adept with sewing other things – like human skin. Daniel had watched her many times and was amazed at how evenly she could sew a stitch, whether on a dress or on him ("Boys," she would often say, "are why thread was invented."). He didn't mind being hurt knowing that his mother was going to fix him up again – it made him feel loved, as was her closing kiss that she promised would "make it all better."

Dr. Sarcophagus beckoned them into his tent. He was tall with skin as white as the wool of a sheep. His head was hairless and it gleamed like his smile – a shark or bear would have been proud to claim it as their own. Daniel noticed that the doctor's clothes were worn and dated: an old tuxedo; pointy, leather shoes; and, in his hand, a scruffy top hat. There was a rectangular table in the middle of the tented room, on the far side of the table an elegant carved wooden chair. Dr. Sarcophagus motioned for them to sit in three less ornate wooden chairs, sat down in his, placed his hat on the table.

And stared at them.

No one uttered a word. Not a sound could be heard from the bustling carnival outside the canvas.

"Daniel." It was one word, but it came as a gunshot in a graveyard, startling all three guests. Their host allowed himself a self-satisfied grin.

No response.

"That is your name, correct? Daniel Lee?" Again, no response. All three were stunned that Dr. Sarcophagus knew the boy's name, and none more than Daniel.

The man turned his attention to Sarah Jean. "How do you feel this fine day, my dear?"

"Um...I...uh...I feel fine. Thank you. Um, how are you?" The last question made Sarah Jean close her eyes, silently chiding her stupidity.

"Oh, I am very well. Did the herbs I brought you help you?"

Sarah Jean avoided his stare. "I…no. I didn't take them yet."

"Ah," he said, knowingly, "there is nothing to fear from them. You must trust me. I am never wrong." Daniel swore that Dr. Sarcophagus glanced at him hungrily before continuing to the woman, "They will give you what you want."

Daniel was confused, but kept quiet. Gregory had told him not to speak unless spoken to. Dr. Sarcophagus turned to Gregory. "Well, Gregory, have you retrieved the water yet?" Gregory was about to answer when the man interrupted him. "No, of course not. And that brings us back to you, Daniel."

Daniel was tired of this. He was on his own because he didn't like being bossed around. He didn't like this carnival and he didn't like Dr. Sarcophagus and he was going to be in charge of himself! "I knew it!" Daniel exclaimed, leaping out of his seat. "You're all the same! You want to run me! No one runs me anymore! I make the rules – my rules!"

Sarah Jean and Gregory gasped. Dr. Sarcophagus said nothing – but Daniel felt like the air in the tent had turned to ice, along with the man's gaze. Dr. Sarcophagus crossed his hands on his lap and, for the first time, spoke without a grin on his lips. "Daniel Lee. You will learn that we all follow rules, whether we know them or not – or like them or not." He spoke to Sarah Jean and Gregory. "If young Master Daniel wishes to stay with our family, he must understand that the privilege comes with responsibilities. He must give as much as he takes – and learn to accept that giving is not taking. Or losing."

He stood up, took his hat and motioned for them to leave. "Sarah Jean and Gregory. You have three days to teach Master Daniel. And Daniel, to be a member of our family means you must be more than a boy with scars. Scars make one tough, but – 'un-pliable'. As I said, you must be giving. Flexible. You must have a talent that adds to our carnival – we have enough 'roadies'. Three days. Then I will decide if you are what I am looking for."

Daniel stared into those glowing sockets and felt there was…caring?

"Yes, what I am looking for…but also what you are looking for."

The trio quietly left. They took a right out of Dr. Sarcophagus' tent and walked past nine more before entering another. This one was not as large as Dr. Sarcophagus', but it was still able to hold a good number of people inside it. There were two cots pushed together in the far corner of the tent and three large chests near them. One of the chests had paper on it and some candles; the other two had nothing on them. There was a third cot in the opposite corner from the first two, but somehow Daniel knew it had never been used.

"This will be your tent while you are a part of our family," said Sarah Jean. "We go to sleep around ten, except when there is a show – then we go to bed once it is all cleaned up." Gregory gestured towards the unused cot, while his wife walked over to one of the chests and pulled out two blankets. She handed them to Daniel and said, "Make up your cot. Then we will talk more."

Daniel nodded. He made his bed robotically. No one had told him to make his bed since his mother – of course, her he always gladly obeyed. Why was he taking orders? Why was he still here? He should have just run – but he looked past the tents to the woods and freedom beyond, and felt discomfited by the thought of being alone. Three days, he thought. It would be nice to have three hots and a cot – for the time being. Then he would be on his way again – on his own.

Things got worse at the Lee household. His father started to drink more – and the more he drank the more the other members of the family suffered. Some days they would meet each other with fresh bruises, welts or cuts. It could be the smallest thing that set him off. One day, Daniel and Samantha were playing jacks on the living room floor, when their father staggered in. "Huh. Playing. World's full of trouble and you're playing!" he grumbled. Right before he stepped on a jack. He yelped in pain and hopped on his good foot. The children couldn't help but giggle – until he stopped hopping and began undoing his belt.

Lillian heard the staccato crack of the belt and her children's wailing. She ran into the room and grabbed her husband's arm. He stopped beating Daniel and Samantha and shoved his wife hard, sending her flying the five feet to the wall. He lunged for her, fist cocked; but before he could unleash his rage, Daniel was off the floor and shoving his mother out of the way. He was the one who took the full brunt of the blow, feeling his father's concrete-like fist plow into his temple, sandwiching his face between it and the wall.

Daniel had grown stronger from the repeated beatings. Tougher. Instead of crumpling to the floor, he fell on one knee and then slowly stood up, defiant, and stared at his father, daring him to hit him again. He took the pain for his mother. He took the pain for love. He wanted his father to see this and stared straight into his eyes. His father, anger spent, could not return the stare. Robert stormed out of the house, out to spend what little money the family had on cheap, backdoor whiskey.

Daniel's mother rushed to him and held him. An ugly bruise had already started to form around the cut that wept blood down his cheek, the only tear that Daniel would allow. His mother ran for her sewing kit and, repeating her oft-spoken words, began stitching up her son.

And, again, he was loved.

The cutting started soon thereafter. One day, Daniel was in his room putting on his pants when he banged into a sharp edge on his bed stand, opening a nasty gash on his thigh. His father was out drinking for a change, while his mother and sister were scrounging for food with their meager allowance. Daniel knew where his mother kept her sewing kit and had watched her nimble fingers so often that he was confident he could match her skill. He threaded the needle the way she did, dipping the end of the thread in his mouth to bring the tip to a fine point. Hesitatingly, the needle hovered over his skin. Daniel took in a deep breath and plunged the tip into his flesh.

The world spun as he his whole body violently shuddered with a sensation more powerful than any blow his father had ever visited upon him. As he pulled the thread through his skin, he could feel his heart race and his breath grow short. Daniel rocked back and forth moaning – not with pain, but with pleasure. He found himself intoning, over and over, with each needle prick, each tug of the thread, "I love you, Daniel…I love you, Daniel…" Suddenly, a new feeling overcame him – a pulsating in his private parts. Then, a wave of supreme heat washed over his entire body and he screamed in unrelenting joy, before collapsing in a heap on the floor.

He lay there, panting, with a feeling of complete satisfaction with himself, with life. It was then that he realized that his underwear was wet. He thought he had urinated; but it wasn't urine – it was something…else. Daniel was scared, embarrassed. He didn't know what had happened. He quickly tied off his stitch and ripped off his underwear, using the cloth to wipe away the blood on his thigh. Grabbing a fresh pair out of his drawer, he put them and his pants on, ran outside and tossed the evidence into a trash heap in an alley.

When he returned home, he ran back upstairs and fell onto his bed in a confusion of emotions and sensations: exhilarated, exhausted, frightened, warm. Whatever had happened, there was one thing for certain. He *liked* it.

That was the beginning of Daniel's new life – a life that would soon be forever changed.

About a month later, Daniel started to notice that his mother was gaining weight. Mostly, it was in her stomach. Finally, on one, rare day when everyone was home and Robert was sober she shared the good news.

"We are going to have a baby!" She was glowing with a huge smile spread across her face. She turned to Samantha, who always looked at her older brother and wished she had a younger sibling, and said, "That means you will be a big sister!"

Samantha was almost as happy as her mother, but Daniel didn't show any of his emotions. He was watching his father. Robert slowly rose from the table and said, "I'm going out." Daniel knew that meant, "Great. More money for another mouth to feed and clothe."

His sister and mother retreated into a happy place of getting everything ready for a new baby. Daniel found his own "happy place" – either taking the punishment from his father for everything, or being in his room with a razor, needle and thread. His mother had long ago let him bathe himself, so she never saw the Lee family history etched in the skin beneath his clothes.

Then, the baby came. He was born at home to avoid the cost of a hospital. A neighbor helped to deliver Timothy James Lee. For the briefest moment, peace and love reigned over the Lee household.

The tragedy struck when Timothy was three months old. Lillian was out and Robert, who had remained surprisingly sober during that time, went to take the baby from his crib. Daniel and Samantha were playing when they heard their father yelling for their mother and his hurried footfalls on the stairs. He appeared carrying a lifeless bundle in his arms and the two children ran to see their brother. His lips were as blue as a summer sky and he was cold to the touch. However, he was still breathing very short, shallow breaths.

Robert yelled for Lillian again.

At that moment, his mother, hearing the yelling as she approached the house, came rushing in, dropping the bag of groceries she had begged for from the produce man. She arrived just in time to hear the baby's last, shallow breath – and the dying sigh of the Lees.

Whatever ember of humanity remained inside Robert Lee was extinguished. Drunken Suffering dethroned Peace in the Lee household. Daniel, Samantha and, most of all, Lillian Lee lived in constant fear of the sound of the door. Not even the comfort of the needle could help Daniel fix the pain.

One morning, Daniel came downstairs and found his father sitting on the floor with a bottle of liquor and his open fishing tackle box. The elder Lee hadn't opened it in years. When he saw Daniel, he called to him in liquorish tones, "C'mere, boy. I have somethin' to give you." Daniel hesitated – but he knew that even the slightest wrong move would unleash the demon inside his father. He sat down. "It's the best gift a father can give his son. I can't keep providin' for you an' the family. You need to fend for yourself." He reached for the bottle and shoved it into Daniel's hands. "First, you're gonna need a drink."

Daniel was terrified. He knew to refuse would be to invite a whipping – even if he'd come to almost welcome them. He also knew what was in the bottle and what it did to his father. But Daniel was also tough – he wasn't going to show weakness to his father. He took a few long pulls and fought back the foulness and stinging, refusing to gag. His father's eyes grew wide and he snatched back the bottle. "So, you're ready to drink, are you? Well, then, you're ready to learn how to provide for yourself."

His father began some bizarre catechism as Daniel felt the warmth of the alcohol course through his veins. "Now, you remember how I took you fishin', right?" Daniel lazily nodded. "Good," said his father. He picked up a knife, a barbed hook and a spool of fishing line out of the box. "Do you remember how I taught you how to make a fire without matches? Good. What 'bout cuttin' fishin' line and tyin' a hook?" Again, Daniel gave a rubbery nod as dizziness made the room wobble. His father drank deeply from his bottle. "Now, as long as you always have a hook, you'll always be ready to fish." Robert reached over and took his son's head in his hands and forced it into his lap. Daniel wanted to struggle, but the liquor had sapped his strength. He looked up out of the side of his eyes and saw his father holding the fishing hook over his head like the priest held up the wafer at church. "Teach a man to fish, and he'll never go hungry," Robert said as he plunged the hook into Daniel's earlobe.

The alcohol dulled, but could not completely mask, the pain. It also could not prevent the eruption of the contents of Daniel's stomach all over his father. Instead of being furious, Robert ferociously laughed, "Welcome to manhood, son!"

Lillian Lee came home after a day and part of the night of begging for whatever food she could and doing backbreaking housecleaning to keep the family afloat. They were all barely eating and she even less to allow her children to have more. Staying away from the house and doing any menial task earned money, and took her mind off of the loss of her baby. She knew, though, that she had two wonderful children who needed her, and the thought always brought her home exhausted and hungry, but smiling.

So, before going to her own room, she did the ritualistic rounds of her children to make sure that they had not been severely injured during a day with their father. Samantha was curled up with her doll, and a cursory examination of her skin revealed no new cuts, bruises or welts. She then went to look in on Daniel. When Lillian bent down to kiss his sleeping ear, she pricked herself on something sharp. In the darkness, her trembling hands reached down and felt the cold, metallic outline of the fishhook in her son's earlobe.

She grabbed her chest as if the hook had gone through her heart – the heart that had been the balloon that kept her aloft above a sea of misery. Now, it was punctured, deflated, empty, lifeless. With the bare remnant of what was left of Lillian Lee, she leaned over and ran her fingers through Daniel's hair. He rolled over and sleepily opened his eyes to see his mother staring at him in the strangest way. She hushed him with the gentle "shh" that had so often soothed his hurts. "Who is Mommy's little doll?" she whispered. Daniel gave her a squinty smile and reached up and touched his nose. "That's right," she said, leaning over and scooping him into her arms. His mother held him tightly and put him back down. She leaned over and said, "Here's a kiss to always make it better." And, with that embrace, she left the room and closed the door, leaving Daniel with his mother's lips on his own as he drifted back to sleep.

Something woke Daniel up early the next morning, just as the sun was rising. He padded downstairs to the kitchen to get a goodbye hug from his mother before she left on her daily search for work. She wasn't there. He wandered through the house, finding his sister still asleep in bed and his father sleeping on the couch. Something made him go to the backyard with the big oak tree at the end by the edge of the fence.

That is where he found her, dangling by her neck from a branch. A chair lay on its side beneath her feet.

Daniel didn't move. He didn't scream. He knew she was dead; but a spark of hope made him reach up. Daniel wanted to turn her around, have her look down and smile at him like it was all a joke. Her body swayed at his touch and slowly twisted around on the rope until he could see her face. That was when he screamed. And screamed. And didn't stop screaming even as his father hit him, even as the fireman cut her down and the policeman questioned his father. The doctor at the hospital gave him something to sleep and told his father that he needed to stay, that the house was not a good place for the boy to be; but his father refused, saying that no one told him what to do with his family and took his son home.

At first, the carnival was like his father, something to be fought, to distrust. Within his first day, he realized that it was more like his mother. The people in the carnival didn't work there, it wasn't a job: it was their home. And, for many, he could tell that it was life itself. He was suspicious why no one attempted to win his trust. He quickly realized why: there was shared understanding that no one was at the carnival by accident – it was where you were meant to be. Daniel could tell that everyone had a story that only found its meaning within the carnival's tents. He found that people referred to each other in familial terms: brother, sister. The carnival was always spoken of reverently, as a sacred mother enveloping them all in her canvas arms. And Dr. Sarcophagus? There was never a question that he was anything less than their saving father.

The second day was a show day; but Daniel was too new to really be much help. So, Sarah Jean and Gregory left him in the tent with some of Gregory's pulp magazines for company. Soon, though, Daniel became bored. He could hear the bustling crowds outside and yearned to be among them; however, he felt bound to stick to his promise to remain inside. Giving up any thoughts of reading, he started exploring the tent, something he had been unable to do when his hosts were around.

It didn't take long for him to realize that, like him, they had very few possessions of note; and certainly nothing of particular interest to keep his time occupied. Sarah Jean's small vanity reminded him of his mother. Lillian Lee was always meticulous about her appearance, and he spent many happy times sitting on her bed while she brushed her hair or prettied up her face.

As he was opening or sniffing various jars, he came across a curious looking bottle. It was a shiny blue with two little arms at the neck and a firmly lodged cork stopper. When he picked it up to examine it more closely, a piece of paper that was stuck to the bottom dropped on the floor. Unfolding it, he saw it was a note that read simply, "Drink and it is yours. Dr. S."

This must be what Dr. Sarcophagus had been talking about to Sarah Jean, he thought. Again, looking about to see if anyone was watching, he uncorked the bottle and brought it to his nose for a sniff. It was indescribable! It smelled like roasted hot dogs, fresh sheets just in from the line, his mother's chicken pot pie, a wood fire in winter – it was as if every scent he had ever loved was in the liquid in the bottle. Daniel could not stop himself – he had to taste it. One sip wouldn't be missed.

He brought the bottle to his mouth. The first drop on his tongue was all that it promised to be – and more. There was nothing he could do – he wanted to stop, but he no longer wanted to taste the drink. He wanted to consume it – no, he wanted it to consume *him*. As if everything that he had ever wanted or needed or hoped for would be at the bottom.

He drank. It seemed like an eternity before the bottle was empty. Daniel felt like he did when his father gave him his first drink of liquor – but this was a different kind of stupor he was in. He felt…relaxed, at peace. He had never felt so peaceful – as if peace was a warm pair of socks you could put on your feet after running shoeless through the snow.

Every bone, muscle and organ felt like it was ready to individually curl up into a ball like a cat on a sunny mantel. Daniel didn't fight the feeling. His rubbery legs were able to get him to his cot where, like a feline, he wrapped himself up in himself and fell asleep – smiling for the first time since his mother kissed him for the last.

The Lee house was nothing more than a roof with walls – the idea of "home" was lying under soft, freshly shoveled earth beneath a cheap marker in the cemetery behind St. Michael's. Daniel and Samantha spent hungry, terrified days and nights, rarely seeing their father and dreading the sound of his footfalls. The two children, always close, now became inseparable. Daniel took on the role of protector for Samantha, taking the blows meant for her just as he had done for his mother. Fortunately, he always had his razor and thread – and, thanks to his father, a needle.

Daniel came home to a quiet house from a day of helping neighbors with chores for a few pennies. His father was nowhere to be found and Samantha failed to rush to the door to greet him as she always did. Fear became palpable. The cut was fresh from the last time Daniel experienced this kind of silence. Still, driven by a sense of duty to his sister, he dashed about the house looking and calling for Samantha. When he got to within a few feet of her bedroom door, he heard a feeble voice utter one word: "Daniel."

Steeling himself, he burst into the room and found it empty. But, again, his name came – and he realized from where. He got down on his hands and knees and looked under the bed. There was a mass of black, blue and red that had been Samantha Lee. He crawled underneath and, against her weak, crying protests, gently pulled her out. He immediately recognized the mark of his father's belt on her face, neck, arms – and that was only the exposed flesh.

"Daniel?" she whispered, "Oh, Daniel. Mommy's here. She says she loves you. I'm going to stay with her for a while." Daniel held her as he started to shake and the tears fell. He choked on his words. Samantha reached up and brushed his cheek. "I love you, Daniel. I'm going – you need to go, too. Goodbye kisses?" Daniel, sopped with tears, leaned over and kissed Samantha gently on her lips, just as his mother always did, and felt her last breath sigh against his.

Daniel put her favorite doll in the crook of her arm and covered her with her blanket. He opened a window and let in the spring air, filled with the flowers she loved, and, he thought, let out her soul to a better place.

He staggered back to his room and sat down with his back against his bed. Reaching behind him, he pulled out his sewing kit from between the mattress and the box spring. Daniel traced the outline of the box and then his lips with his fingers, remembering the last touch of the two people who were his world. He would never lose them again. He opened up the box and began.

When Robert Lee came home, the house was dark except for a flickering glow in the front room window. Opening the door he yelled, "Daniel! Samantha! I better not –"

And stopped.

There, sitting cross-legged on the floor, was Daniel, surrounded by fires burning in Lillian Lee's prized cooking pots. Robert saw that the boy was wearing nothing but a pair of shorts, cut from his pants. His anger was tempered by the weirdness of the scene. Daniel said, "I learned my lessons well, father. Do you like my fires?"

Robert's eyes began to adjust to the light. For the first time in the Lee house, it was Robert who screamed in fear and pain. He saw Daniel's skin. The tracks of cuts, scars, stitches. A history of suffering told by Robert and written by Daniel, etched on his fleshly parchment. Robert slowly walked towards Daniel who was still sitting on the floor. As he got closer, he saw the final horror: his son's mouth was a crosshatch of stitches running all along his lips.

Standing above Daniel, Robert could only muster a stuttered, "What's the meaning of this?" Daniel did not look at him – he was staring straight ahead, through his father and out the door. His father no longer existed – he might as well have sprung miraculously from Lillian Lee's womb. It was time.

Searing pain embraced Robert Lee's body. His head crazily tottered on his neck as he looked down to see blood gushing down his son's hands and arms, enveloping the hilt of the knife – Robert's knife – that had been thrust upwards through his genitals and into his groin. The elder Lee crumpled to the floor, knocking aside three of the fire pots and setting the carpeting ablaze. To ensure that he would be untroubled, he took the knife and slammed it, one stab at a time, through his father's shoulders. His father screamed like a girl. Daniel kneeled above him and removed the fishing hook from his ear. Robert gurgled something incomprehensible as Daniel threaded the line into the hook, just as his father had taught him. Holding the hook and line just above Robert's mouth, Daniel stared into his father's terrified eyes and coldly said, "Teach a man to fish, and he'll never go hungry."

Daniel awoke to his name being yelled. As he came out of his haze he saw Sarah Jean standing over him, with Gregory quickly arriving by her side. Reflexively, Daniel went to stretch as he awoke – and realized that his arms were tucked neatly behind his upper back, his elbows tucked beneath his neck and his hands resting on alternate shoulders. "Call Dr. Sarcophagus!" Sarah Jean shrieked, shaking Gregory. "Tell him that Daniel somehow dislocated his shoulders!" Gregory turned – and stopped as he watched Daniel, it could only be called "unwind" himself, stretch and get out of bed as if nothing had happened. Daniel was more mystified than horrified. In fact, after the initial surprise, he felt as if this was how he had always been.

It was when he got up that Sarah Jean saw the blue bottle on the bed, where it had rested underneath Daniel as he slept.

Sarah Jean dragged Daniel, with the bottle, to see Dr. Sarcophagus – to Hell with his rule of not being bothered until noon on the day after a performance. When they got to his tent, they were met by someone Daniel had never seen before: a man with no face. The man put his hand on Sarah Jean's shoulder and she swatted it away. "Get out of the way, Raphael," Sarah Jean growled, "we need to see Dr. Sarcophagus – now."

"It's alright," said a voice from within the tent, "I've been expecting them." Daniel realized that the man had no ears either. So, how did he…? The man opened the tent and beckoned them in.

Dr. Sarcophagus was sitting at the table in exactly the same clothes and position in which Daniel had first met him. "So, Daniel," he said with that inordinately toothy smile, "Have you come to show me something and for me to give my decision?"

Sarah Jean wanted to explode at the man; but there was something about his expression and bearing that made it impossible for her to do anything but say, "Doctor, Daniel drank my herbs – and now look at him." She gave Daniel a hard nudge in the small of his back, sending him forward. Dr. Sarcophagus looked at him and asked, "Well?" Daniel was getting angry. He was being bossed around – it was like old times. He didn't like "old times." He was ready to leave when something stayed his hand – it was the memory of how the carnival made him feel during the last three days.

So, he pushed down his anger and decided to show the good doctor something he would never forget. He sat down on the floor and began folding his body in on itself a limb at a time. Daniel kept staring at the man, as if daring him to say something, be horrified or show some emotion. Instead, it was only Sarah Jean who gasped – had she not become so inured to the strange, she would have fallen to the dusty floor in a swoon. The man just sat there with his smile growing broader as Daniel grew smaller.

Daniel sat in his human ball, unmoving. Dr. Sarcophagus stood up and walked over to him. He pulled up his pant legs and got down on his haunches to be almost eye-to-eye with Daniel. "So, you have spent the latter part of your short existence exactly like this: cocooned, protecting yourself from being harmed, from allowing anyone in or providing an opening to your trust. But just as no one can get in, neither can you get out. Daniel," the man said commandingly as he stood up, "it is time to come out and to let the world back in. You are forgiven. Forgive yourself. Now."

An animal-like howl of anguish filled every fold of the canvas. Daniel unspooled like a tightly wound spring, releasing all of the tension in his body, in his soul. He lay on the floor of the tent sobbing, releasing a torrent of tears that threatened to sap every drop of moisture from his body. Sarah Jean dropped to her knees and pulled him to her, holding him tighter than anything she had ever held before. "Daniel, don't cry. It's going to be okay. I promise. I'm here to take care of you. I'll always be here to take care of you." Daniel looked up at her through his tears and sobbed, "Do you promise, Mommy?" Sarah Jean felt her own tears well up and spring forth from inside her. She rocked him back and forth, clutching him to her breast, saying, "I promise. Mommy promises."

Dr. Sarcophagus left them there, walking towards the back chamber of the tent. As he entered the darkened gloom, he glanced back, put on his hat and softly said as he closed the canvas flap behind him, "Show's over, folks."

TENT 2

BUT NOW I SEE
Jeffrey Stundel

Night. To him, it held no romance. The salt of desperation sweat. The reek of cheap, heeled-out cigarettes. He could taste it all. Smell it all. All of it, rising above the dust that enveloped and choked everything like filthy, powdered sugar. Inescapable. Under your nails, in your hair, in every exposed orifice – and some that weren't.

The alternative? Day. More sugar – still not sweet – of desiccation and perspiration coalescing into molasses on skin. A skyward face seeking the coolness of raindrops, only greeted by the drifting, biting grit. And always the people. The pushing, plodding, filthy, odiferous masses driven like elephants on a barren African plain in search of a watering hole. The groans, like the baying of beasts, when the trail ended at a dry riverbed.

A smack to the head.

"Stop daydreamin', boy – before I give you somethin' to dream about you ain't gonna want to dream!"

The dull thudding in his head faded while the man ranted. He closed his mind's door to the sensation and settled in a comfortable chair inside. This was the only place he had to himself. It always amazed him that others never turned inwards to escape, choosing rather to seek escape out there – where it would never come. No sanctuary. No Eden. Just barren, dusty desolation at the end of every mile.

"God dammit, boy!" bellowed the man. "Sheeit! You done made me balspheme th' Lord's name! You'll get His right justice through me!"

The Reverend Clemson promised Eden was to be found in the pages of the Good Book. He needed to open people's eyes to the signposts clearly printed therein. Blind, they were. Stubborn like mules. His words fell like lashes driving them forward toward salvation. And the people took their well-earned punishment – didn't the good reverend say that they were being paid the wages of sin? That those sins were what turned the world into a blighted, burning Hell?

Certainly, anyone could feel their desperation. Huddling together, pushing forward to reach out to the reverend for his healing touch. And then their horror when the reverend revealed him with an ecstatic flourish as the embodiment of transgression in flesh. The bodies writhing like sheep in a pen, bleating in terror as the reverend's angry admonitions rained down upon them like flaming hammers, beating them into the submission of promised purity. And when words didn't work, his bullwhip was the ideal motivator.

He felt pain slice across his back, lash its tongue to his flesh and, sliding away, lick out a groove of searing agony. The vibrations of the reverend's bellowed exhortations were so thick on the air that you could pick out the words with your fingers. "Boy, I'm gonna peel you like an apple! You ain't gonna lie down for a week when I'm done with you!"

The beatings came more regularly now as his audiences – and his pockets from their pitiful pennies – grew equally thinner. Perhaps the reverend blamed him for the diminished returns. Maybe he was just trying to vent his frustrations. Then, again, the truth was evident to even a blind man – or woman.

Sarah held him in her arms after placing a salve on his back and wrapping his wounds. In the darkness, he didn't need to see her to know her beauty. Many nights they lay together as he traced her face with his fingertips, breathed in her scent above the dust. She could see him for more than him – in her blindness, her perceptions were more acute than a seeing person's.

As she cradled him in her arms, he could feel the music coming from her. Sarah's gift was her voice. When she sang *Amazing Grace*, one was certain the sky would release a torrent of life-giving angels' tears onto the parched earth. Even now, her merely humming the tune sent cooling chills to his wounds – not just the ones on his back, but every hurt he had ever received. It was always like this when they were together. He reached up and brought her head to his naked chest, to turn his body into her instrument as her vibrato tingled over every inch of his being. And when she climbed on top of him and put him inside her, he was saved.

A new day, a new town. Or what amounted to one. An agglomeration of rickety trucks, tents, wagons, humans and animals – although it was getting harder every day to tell the latter two apart.

But he was always the animal. And the reverend never let him forget it. Sarah traveled in the cab of the truck with the reverend. He was left to swelter in the heat of the closed canvas of the bed with the bare necessities of their traveling salvation show and what few personal possessions they – or, more precisely, the reverend – had.

Cut off from the two other travelers, he could still sense the palpable lust thrusting forth from the reverend toward Sarah. It disgusted him. It tasted like rotting bile in his mouth. Sarah never had to tell him when the reverend had made one of his advances. He could tell at night when he held her and she held him back more tightly, as if trying to burrow into him for safety. Thus far, it was nothing more than leering lechery – but he could tell that the time was not far off before it would turn physical.

"C'mon, boy. It's almost showtime." The reverend gave him a solid kick in the behind to get him into position for the show. "Don't you give me that face, boy," the reverend growled, "You're damn lucky you got me to look after you – you think you'd last two seconds out there? Sheeit. They'd laugh at you, then they'd beat you and, if you got lucky, they'd kill you with a quick lynchin'." Another kick in the behind. "So don't you forget it and just keep bein' your ugly self!"

He'd lost count of the beatings, great and small, since he was born, beginning with the one administered by his father. First, his father in a drunken rage beat his mother claiming that she had whored with another man because, "I could NEVER be responsible for THAT!" Then when he turned his attention to the baby, he was too distracted wielding his workboot to notice his wife behind him with a cast-iron frying pan. The police found her standing at the stove, singing softly to herself, spattered in blood and brains, holding her baby over one shoulder and frying what looked like eggs.

His mother went to an insane asylum. He went to an orphanage.

It was at the orphanage that he met others like him. Where he met Sarah. Where he received the name that others rarely used. And where, as he grew, he built his home inside.

The first room came by accident. He was eating breakfast with some other residents when he was hit in the nose and mouth with a spoonful of oatmeal. He sat there motionless while the offender laughed. His first instinctive reaction was to lick the oatmeal off of his lips. He could feel the room grow cold as he did so – and so did the owner of the cereal catapult.

Suddenly, he burst forth, as if reborn, into a world of vivid sensation. In a large room filled with an endless array of burgeoning bookcases a clock ticked in the corner. An enormous bay window was open, letting in the afternoon sun, sounds of birds and the sweetest autumn breeze he had ever smelled. His senses overwhelmed, he staggered into a large, cushioned leather armchair, where he collapsed in a half swoon. But everything seemed to be as it always had been, as he always had been.

His reverie was broken by a strange sound from outside. He went to the window and, when he looked out, in the distance, he could see a small figure writhing on the ground, clawing at its face and head, beneath a giant oak tree.

"Woe be to you, sinners! Your sins of greed, of flesh – y'all be th' ones who brung this misery to yourselves – upon us all!" The sheep bleated in weak assent. They swayed under the weight of their guilt. "I'm talkin' to you fornicators! You!" the reverend screamed, pointing to a filthy young woman, "I can smell th' lust upon your loins! Whose seed is that dryin' there, huh? How can you lift your hand to Jesus when you're on all fours ruttin' like an animal?"

The woman groaned and covered her face in shame. The others shied away from her, leaving her alone in a small clearing, afraid that her sin would infect them all. The reverend's face was red, eyes bulging as he screeched, "Don't y'all shun her! Don't y'all shun her! Y'all are guilty! 'For all have sinned and fall short of th' glory of God!' Repent! Repent! Or burn in this fiery Hell for all time! See now your sins made of flesh – see th' wrath of th' Lord that's upon y'all!"

Suddenly, the reverend's hand was through the bed sheet that served as a curtain, gripping him and frantically pulling him forth. The ground shook from the panicked, trampling of feet and the volcanic eruption of stark fear and of a unified anguished appeal to God for redemption.

The reverend beamed down upon his flock in triumph.

The show was over. And penitence was to be found not within one's soul, but within one's purse. One by one, the people, staggering from the incessant verbal and visual spiritual blows, shuffled to the reverend for his grace and pardon – which he gladly gave for a small donation. Sarah's voice floated over all, the notes of *Amazing Grace* falling on the somewhat poorer parishioners like soothing snowflakes.

He, on the other hand, was behind the curtain, back in his home.

No one quite understood what had happened during breakfast that day. Two things, though, were thereafter forever changed: Willy, the teenager who threw the oatmeal, had mutilated himself so badly that he lost his vision and sank into a state of near infantilism; the victim of the attack, however, seemed to grow perceptibly more intelligent as the days after the attack progressed.

Every day, he would sneak off to a quiet place in the orphanage where he knew he would not be found. There, he would return to that magical room and slowly teach himself to read. Time worked very differently inside than outside. What passed for hours in the former were but moments in the latter. As he spent more time inside and learned more from the books, he found that he could adjust the environment to suit his mood: day, night, summer, winter.

Soon, he had gone from being a novice reader to a voracious autodidact with an ever-expanding intellect and hunger for knowledge. One day, after having completed his fifth re-reading of the entire library, he threw himself into the chair and turned his head to gaze out the window. He had chosen a late spring morning, and the smell of fresh, dewy grass was intoxicatingly maddening. It was then that he decided it was time to do what he had yet to attempt: leave the room.

He had always thought it odd that there was not a single door, with the only form of ingress or egress being the window. He felt he could make the leap to the large oak tree just outside, clamber down and more fully explore his interior world. Standing on the sill, the distance suddenly seemed a yawning chasm; but he realized that he had exhausted what he could learn in the library and needed something more. His insurmountable desire for knowledge overcoming his fear, in a frantic leap he hurtled across the gap – only to find himself back in the outside.

"Yep, we done pretty good today," chuckled the reverend. "Not as pretty as you, li'l lady," he added, rubbing the small of Sarah's back, his hand lingering just at the top of her buttocks, "but it'll sure do." The reverend turned to him and slyly asked, "What? You don't like it when I do this?" and started caressing her again. Suddenly, his smile faded. "What're you givin' me that face for?" he growled darkly. "Put that danged tongue back in your mouth! Don't you sass me, boy, or else I'll give you another lickin'!"

The reverend's demeanor once again turned nastily playful, "Well now. I guess I should stop, or else you might take offense and do something about it, heh?" The reverend gave Sarah a slap on the behind that crackled in the air. He burst into raucous laughter at his own cleverness and walked off to count his own wages of sin. The old man always enjoyed this part of the game, thinking that only he was playing. If only he knew what was to be found in a book in a very secret library: "All war is based on deception."

Other rooms followed. Shortly after his failed attempt to flee the library, he learned the secret behind gaining them – and the cost.

It was Christmas – or what the orphanage could muster for a Christmas from charitable donations. For him, it was a paradise: the smell of simmering cider, the taste of warm sugar cookies from the oven, the frosty bite of a snowball on gloveless hands.

Someone thought it would be quaint and amusing to hang mistletoe – even though most of the residents were hardly into their teens. As he was standing beneath it, a young girl, egged on by her friends, walked over to him and gave him a kiss. She thought it would be funny – run back giggling to her equally giggling friends.

She spent Christmas strapped to a bed to prevent her from tearing out her other eye.

And a boy who had snatched a cookie from him that he was eating and devoured it himself was dead by the end of New Years week after ripping off his ears and tunneling up to his wrists into the yawning cavities left behind.

Meanwhile, he had a bedroom and music room to explore.

He sat in the dark alone, thinking of Sarah. Tonight was an evening when the reverend was using her vocal talents to pad his pockets.

No one at the orphanage quite knew what to make of the growing number of incidents – "accidents," as they were referred to in reports to the orphanage's governing board. The fear was so thick he could taste it. He could feel the residents and staff withdraw from him. As they did, he withdrew into his mansion inside. A hodgepodge of experience with only one unifying element: they were all his.

One day, he was practicing his self-imposed piano lesson when he was pulled out of his musical reverie by a body sprawling across his. A young girl about his age had gone exploring in what she thought was a little used part of the orphanage – but discovered that she wasn't the first one there.

They had both been knocked over, and she was lying across his chest. The scent of her breath was more beautiful than the flowers that bloomed outside of his kitchen. In trying to get up, her hands found her way to his face and, reading the story to be found thereupon, recognized her stumbling partner from the stories going around the orphanage.

Her initial trepidation was evident in the trembling of her hands upon his face. And yet, she continued her perusal, growing more comfortable with each pass. Soon, he found a warmth in her touch that made him suddenly self-conscious. He recoiled from her and tried to get up, to run. For some reason, though, she gently held his face – and for the first time, he felt Sarah's song. It was more beautiful than anything he had played on the Victrola – it wasn't a song to be heard, but in which to be enveloped.

He could sense something was very wrong. There was a metallic scent on the air. It was bitter on his tongue. Blood. It mingled with recognizable and unrecognizable sweat, dirt.

Sarah.

He leaped to his feet and ran out into the night – but stopped not more than a few yards from the tent.

She was lying on the ground, barely breathing. He could hear the painful, stuttered heaves as lungs stretched agonizingly against broken ribs. Her body was slick with a muddy miasma of blood, sweat – and man fluid. She released a smothered, guttering scream as he picked her up to carry her back to the tent. She was more naked than clothed, and what flesh he felt was covered in gashes, bruises – a broken wrist bone jutting through her skin.

He began to minister to her as she did so many times to him. He could cry no tears as he explored her body that read like an encyclopedia of inhuman violation: a smashed nose, shattered cheekbone, swollen shut eyes, disjointed jaw, broken ribs and wrist. Every inch of her was crosshatched with wounds of every nature. He was sickened when he felt her clawed, bitten breast and a nipple flapped over, hanging by a sliver of skin. Sarah incoherently blubbered. He couldn't stop himself. He had to check. She weakly swatted at him with her good hand and shook her head from side to side to make him stop – even now trying to protect him.

Her female parts – she howled in agony when he touched her. The reverend was here. And others. She writhed from the torture – physical, emotional. He wanted to hold her, to comfort her, but did not for fear that it would only cause her more pain. He did not know what to do. No book could prepare him for this. No learning. Sarah convulsed and raggedly coughed. A gout of blood spurted from her lips, spraying his face, baptizing him with her.

The reverend.

They were sixteen when he "adopted" them. He had not a clue as to what the reverend said to the orphanage to get them released to his custody. Perhaps they saw him as the simple, country preacher he professed to be, trying to innocently save their souls for God. Perhaps they were getting too old and the staff was happy to find someone to take them in to make room for younger children. He always suspected that it wasn't a question of being too old, but being too odd.

He and Sarah had become inseparable. She was how he saw the outside world. They had a way of communicating with each other that required nothing more than a touch – and with that touch, she helped him make a life here. He was terrified the first time they kissed – but nothing happened, except pure ecstasy. Later, he experimented and gained his final room.

When they found the boy who had tried to rape him, his hands were reduced to wet, red, Spanish moss hanging from bony branches and his eye sockets filled with glass shards.

He had smashed a window, crumbled the shattered pieces in his hands and ground the coarse crystalline powder into his eyes.

That, he felt, was the final straw that sent them into the arms of the Reverend Clemson and his salvation sideshow.

The reverend was never pleasant, and he always treated Sarah like an angel and him like a devil. They immediately became a part of his Sunday ecumenical extravaganzas: him, the mortal expression of the Pit; her, the voice of the Heavenly Host. And he treated them before, during and after accordingly. But it wasn't until after the dust turned everything into a choking Hell, sending them chasing after the reverend's scattered flock, that his innate cruelty found its brutal outlet.

The warmth was ebbing from Sarah's body. He traced every inch of her, memorializing her in his mind, making for her a shrine. He swore, as he felt her last breath gurgle from her cracked and bloody lips, that his goddess would have a worthy sacrifice with which to dedicate her temple.

He smelled his fingers. The reverend. Others he could not place. He knew that this was the reverend's doing. He also knew that the reverend would denounce him in the morning. "Look at him! What'd you expect from an animal that looks like that?!" He would get the lynching the reverend had always promised.

The hard earth yielded. You are dust, and to dust you shall return.

"Where is she?!" raged the reverend. His whip had already eaten of his body. "You know! I know you know! You ain't as dumb as you let on, now are you?!" The ground shook with the reverend's enraged stamping. "Did you kill her? Huh? Drive her away? She talkin' with th' staties?" The reverend brought the butt end of the whip down on his head. "C'mon, boy! Use that heathen tongue of yours and tell me! Tell me!" The reverend's voice was like the piping of a steaming teapot as he repeated the blow.

A halo of pain engulfed him. But he stood fast. Emotionless. Blank.

"We gots a show to do, boy – I ain't got time to diddle around! For th' last time," the reverend foamed, "WHERE'S YOUR FUCKIN' WHORE?!"

The reverend balled up his fist and cocked his arm.

He smiled.

The reverend was before a sellout crowd wielding his words like a holy flail falling on the backs of the massed masochists. They begged for his verbal flagellation. Moaned when the spoken leather cracked against their deserving, sinful skin.

The sermon's topic was his favorite. "'For th' lips of an adulteress drip with honey, and her speech is smoother than oil!'" the reverend raged. "'But in th' end, she's as bitter as gall – and as sharp as a double-edged sword!'" He stalked the stage like a wild man, his angry spittle spraying forth from his lips – and the crowd felt as if anointed with holy water. He picked his usual target and accusingly held forth his hands towards her. "Here! Look at her! Bosoms flyin' free and easy! Why, I do believe she's wearin' makeup! She's sinnin' while we're seekin' the Lord's salvation!" Groans of "Harlot!" and "Whore of Bablyon!" rose up in the thick morning air.

The reverend, swept up in his own ecstatic fury, jumped in front of the woman, grabbed her by the shoulders and shook her like a rag doll screaming, "'Like a gold ring in a pig's snout – that's th' good lookin' woman who shows herself like that!'" He hurled her away and got back in front of the crowd. "Y'all are pigs! Y'all are all sows and hogs gruntin' and sweatin' in your sties!"

Behind the sheet, he waited. Would it work? Would his anger be enough to make it work? He had never tried – never wanted to try. But now – now was different. Without Sarah, he was truly lost, truly fumbling in the world, truly apart from the rest of mankind. Alone.

Another person caught the reverend's eye – and wallet. "You there – in th' back! In your fancy duds. You think you're better than everyone else? 'All is vanity!' And vanity leads to lust and lust leads to sinnin'!" The reverend, again worked up into a froth, rumbled, "And by th' looks of you, you're th' biggest sinner here!" The man in the top hat stood unperturbed. He merely gazed at the reverend from beneath the wide brim, his eyes meeting the reverend's – gleaming, as if in challenge – his wry, toothy smile, etched with cunning. Only the reverend's onrushing avalanche of fury was enough to sweep him away from that face.

Returning his anger to the masses, he exhorted, "Y'all ever look in th' mirror? Ever see yourselves for what y'all are? Well, here! See! See!" The reverend reached through the sheet and felt sharp pain coursing through his hand. With a yelp he pulled it back, the knuckles raw and bleeding where teeth had dug into them. Instinctively, he shoved them in his mouth.

Piano music brought the reverend back to his senses. He was in the back of a large, darkened room. In front of him were rows of people sitting with their backs to him listening to the pianist playing before them. The reverend's eyes were still getting acquainted with the darkness as he walked down the aisle towards the music.

As he drew nearer, the pianist began looking damnably familiar; but the reverend couldn't place him. The player finished his piece and, as the last echoes of the notes died, he composed himself, stood up and turned to face the reverend.

"Welcome, Reverend Clemson. So good of you to join us. Won't you have a seat and enjoy the concert?" He was a young man – no more than his early twenties – with jet-black hair and the most piercing coal-like eyes the reverend had ever seen. And that voice – deep, commanding, steady.

"Who th' Hell are you – and what th' Hell's this place? Who're these folks?" the reverend demanded. "Why, reverend," responded the man coolly, "Don't you know who I am? You should." The reverend looked at him confused. "Come now," said the man, "We've known each other for years. I'm insulted."

"I don't know what you're playin' at, young feller – but I ain't in th' mood for games!"

"Well," replied the man, "Perhaps you will recognize me better like this." Before the reverend's ever-widening eyes, the young man started to change. His eyelids fused to his cheeks, leaving nothing but smooth, pink bulges. His ears disappeared and his hair grew ragged and shaggy across his scarred face. And from out of his mouth came a long, sinewy tongue, lapping at the air like a paper streamer in the breeze.

The reverend screamed.

"No! It can't be! Sweet Jesus, Almighty! This ain't real! Y'all ain't real!"

A wry smile played across the man's lips. "Oh, but it is real. And I? I am very real. And so is she." At that, the sound of singing came from the back of the room. A figure emerged from the darkness – a figure with the most beautiful voice anyone had ever heard.

The reverend tore at his hair, screeching. "No! Keep her away from me! You – y'all are devils – that's what y'all are! I'll send you back to th' infernal depths, I will!"

As the woman neared, the reverend screamed again. She was a bleeding corpse. Half naked, covered in rags, skin flayed – arms outstretched. "Come, reverend," she sweetly intoned, "Don't you want to finish what you started – before I fought you, hurt you and you turned me over to those men to do to me what you couldn't?"

Staggering backwards, the reverend tripped over himself as he tried to escape. "Get away from me, you harlot from Hell! I cast you out and back to Hell where you came from!

The man walked towards him, beckoning the audience to come forward. "No, reverend. It is you who belongs in Hell. You who cheated gullible, desperate people out of their money. You who cheated two individuals out of their youth." The man's face returned to its original form. The eyes burning like twin furnaces. His voice, basso, reverberating like a pronouncement from God. "You who stole my life. My love. My eyes in your world."

The people moved closer. The reverend could hear them speaking.

"Ye cannot serve God and Mammon."

"Thou art weighed in the balances, and art found wanting."

"For they have sown the wind, and they shall reap the whirlwind."

The reverend was hysterical. He cried out for God's mercy.

The man sat down again at the piano and asked the woman, "Sarah, my love. A song for the reverend?" Sarah kissed him on the forehead and replied, "Raphael, my heart, you know the song."

He began to play.

And she began to sing.

"Amazing grace. How sweet the sound. That saved a wretch like me..."

The reverend dropped to his knees, then on the ground on his side, his hands over his ears. The singing was filling his ears with boiling oil. He ripped at them to let it flow out.

"I once was lost, but now am found."

Now, his eyes were burning like red-hot iron balls in his sockets. He writhed in agony – clawing at them.

His last sight was the crowd of people of all ages coming into the light with empty, bloody holes from whence their eyes had been gouged, gory stumps where once had been ears.

And they joined their voices with Sarah's.

"Was blind, but now I see!"

On the outside, the crowd was wailing, trampling itself, crying and flying as fast as it could – to seek salvation in the dust from whence they came.

Behind them, the reverend, head bathed in scarlet gore, held up two, shaking, ensanguined fists, dripping with scarlet jelly, raised to God on High, shrieking, "I see! I see!"

Epilogue

These damned carnies, thought the man in the suit as he wandered through the tented lanes. Damned filthy tramps. He sniffed at the tattered canvas and cursed as, distracted, he stepped into something unmentionable. If they were going to come in and stink up his town, run their flim-flams and swindle his people out of their money – Hell, that was his job – well, then, by God, he was going to see to it that he made it up at the carnival's expense.

The man in the black top hat beckoned him to come closer. "Please, councilman. Sit. Now, tell me again about these fees. I'm quite certain I don't remember these the last time we passed through here."

Before the councilman could speak, he noticed a figure emerge from the shadows to stand beside his host. Glancing beside him, the man chuckled, "Oh, you needn't be concerned. Raphael is just here to observe and listen."

"Uh," stammered the councilman. "But – I – well, I don't mean to sound indelicate, but…"

"Ah, yes," the man responded reassuringly, "you are referring to Raphael's 'shortcomings'. Please accept my apology. Tenderness often leads one to misspeak. I rescued him from a lynching and now, well, he feels bound to be with me at all times." The man patted Raphael's leg. "And I feel a certain fatherly protectiveness towards him in return. So. As you were saying?"

The councilman was unnerved by the blank, expressionless visage. He tried to speak, but could only muster a catch in his throat. The top-hatted man extended a concerned hand. "Oh dear. Are you having difficulty breathing? I'm afraid I must apologize again. So much dust gets trapped in this," he said, gesturing about him with a lazy wave of this arm, "and we are so used to it." He turned to the man next to him and, holding his hands, made a gesture of pouring water into a glass. "One moment, councilman. Raphael will return with some water."

Raphael returned with a glass of water and offered it to the councilman. The latter's hand shook as he took it, spilling its contents on his pants. The man in the top hat seemed to give a mischievous, knowing smile as the water was taken, drunk and the glass returned to its bearer. "Now, then," said the councilman, nervously clearing his throat, "There is so much that goes into running a town – and that 'much' is money." The talk of cash and the thought of getting it from these freaks restored the councilman's swagger. "Why, by God, if you could only see what I go through to make ends meet!"

The man tiredly removed his top hat, revealing a bald, beaming head. He dusted off the brim, turned to his silent sentinel and, touching his hand, said, "Well, then, Raphael, my angel, why don't we take a look?"

Raphael nodded in assent and brought the councilman's glass to his lips.

TENT 3

THE RAVEN MASTER
Cindy Livingston

Summer, 1927. Raleigh, North Carolina

"Father?"

The question was preceded by a knock at the door, as it always did, in the darkness of the evening morn. The man inside was awake, as he always was, and had been expecting the guest. "Come in, Branna," he responded. He answered softly enough to comfort a child, but loudly enough that his voice would carry to the outside.

The door creaked open and in from the damp heat came a small form tightly wrapped in a black cape. It was too hot for such attire; but the man understood the reluctance of his adopted daughter to be more lightly clothed, she who was one of a number of family members who were only residents and not performers.

A pale, girlish face peered out from the hood. She was much, much older than a child; and yet carried herself with a child's bearing.

"Did it happen again, my little faerie?" the man gently asked. He replaced the quill pen into its holder, closed his secretary and swiveled on his wooden chair to fully face his guest. She nervously stamped her feet, not knowing what to do – despite many such visits – and the man beckoned her to sit on his bed.

He always called her his "little faerie." In truth, it was an apt term of endearment: she was small, almost supernaturally beautiful – when she chose to be revealed – and odd, magical events always seemed to be a part of her experience. And yet, there was a darkness beneath it all, just like the black cloth within which she chose to conceal herself.

She sighed as she sat down and pulled back her cowl to reveal her head. Long, mahogany locks spilled down her shoulders as she shook them free. Her steel grey eyes were accented by thin, dark eyebrows that seemed to fade into the sides of her head. Her skin was alabaster pale and smooth. If she had not chosen to remain a relative hermit, the man was quite certain he would have considerable difficulties with his male patrons.

"Father," she began, "long ago, you told me that you were bound by a promise to raise me as your own. No daughter could love a father more if she were his own flesh and blood." She turned her head away, fighting back tears and the catch growing in her voice. Composing herself, she turned and fixed her gaze on the man. "I feel, though, that I belong somewhere…else. Every time I look in the mirror and see…well, you know what I see…I feel as if I need to leave and go – somewhere…just not this…world."

The man stood up and settled next to her. He put his arm around her and, looking deep into her eyes, said, "I also told you that there would come a time when you would seek answers and that I would give them – when I thought you were ready. And I think now is that time."

Winter, 1851. London.

Night. The cowl and cloak were ill protection against the freezing rain that wept down upon me – upon the small, wrapped body squirming in my arms. As I leaned over the stonework wall of the bridge, I closed my eyes, exhaled and ever so slightly loosened my grip. It was time to let it go. To let go of the horror that had befallen me.

The click of a metal-tipped cane and the stamping of sturdy footfalls shook me from my thoughts. My hands reflexively tightened around the bundle. The gaslight revealed a tall man bent over against the rain. I breathed a sigh of relief. Not a constable.

His step was slow and sure – and much to my distress, not in a hurry to be out of the foul winter weather. I would have to wait until he passed to finish my deed. But instead of passing, he halted beside me.

"Good evening, sir," he said, in an accent that was not of England, tipping his tall, black top hat to me, as the rain sloughed off of it to mingle with the puddles at our feet. I had never seen skin so pale and white, and I wondered uncomfortably if the gentleman had ever seen a ray of sunshine in his life. As if sensing my apprehension, he smiled at me baring an eerie array of teeth.

A chill crept up my spine and I clutched my package closer to my chest, suddenly grateful for its warmth – and guilty for the gratitude. With the cold rain now drizzling down my neck as I craned to look up at him, I politely nodded back.

"'d evening, sir," I managed to stutter, trying to keep my teeth from chattering. He placed his hat back atop his head and asked, all too pleasantly and without a hint of irony, "Lovely night isn't it?" He reached into his cloak and deftly pulled out a card, extending it to me with a white-gloved hand. As I struggled to find a hand with which to accept it, he shook his head and chuckled, as if embarrassed by his lapse in judgment. "Oh dear. Please forgive me – your hands are full. Here, let me hold it while you read my card."

Suddenly, I was angry. Angry at what drove me to this bridge at night in an icy, pissing rain. Angry at this odd stranger who was preventing me from the task I so desperately needed to complete. "Good sir," I said, trying to keep my voice even, "I'm afraid this bundle is too precious to place in another's hands."

The man nodded in what seemed to be amusement. "But of course. Please excuse my impertinence. As you may have surmised, I am a stranger here – on business."

He bowed deeply and I caught a glimpse of the head of his cane. It was topped with an elaborately carved ivory skull with emerald eyes. This was indeed a man of wealth and privilege. I looked back on his face and his fixed gaze filled me with the urge to entrust in him all of my secrets.

And then I saw him greedily eye the bundle I clutched. "You know," he said softly, encouragingly, "my business is *most* discreet." He took a step nearer, now standing awkwardly close. He lowered his face to mine and said, in a hushed, compelling tone, "I may be able to offer assistance."

I backed away slightly, not entirely comfortable with my close proximity to this stranger. Again, I found myself stuttering, "I - I assure you, I am not in need of assistance, sir."

The man stood up and released a guffaw out of character with the evening's silence, shattering the whispering rain. Composing himself, he said with a knowing smile, "Oh, I think you are – or else you wouldn't be here, now would you?"

I tried to fight his eyes, but I could only mutter, "I – I work nearby," cocking my head towards the Tower of London across the Thames, "in the Tower. I'm the raven master."

"Indeed!" the stranger replied with what seemed mocking admiration. "A most fascinating profession! Perhaps it would be a warm, dry place to discuss your quandary."

I felt in his thrall. Helpless. I nodded in agreement.

I laid the bundle down on my bed and turned to look at him. He removed his rain-drenched overcoat and hung it on the nearby coat rack. He took a seat in my tattered wingback chair, tucking his long, black coat tails beneath him. He leaned forward and, with a waved flourish of his hand, said, "Proceed."

I began my story.

Legend has it that if the ravens of the Tower of London were to leave, the Tower would fall and a great tragedy would befall England. In deference to the legend, six ravens are lodged and cared for here. But there is a secret long passed down from one raven master to another, that there is a seventh raven, with unclipped wings, which calls the Tower home. She comes and goes as she pleases and must never be caught.

With each hearing of the tale of the seventh raven, my curiosity burned ever brighter. What madness insinuated itself into my brain, I cannot say; but even though I knew it was wrong, I could not pull my thoughts from the gnawing need to capture her. Then, one day, I could no long contain myself. I went to the docks and bought a net.

One evening, as the sun was almost setting, I caught sight of her perched alone between two crenulations. I was able to stealthily approach as she was basking unaware in the late-day beams. I proved her sense of safety wrong as I threw the net and, in one, swift motion yanked it back with my prize inside.

She struggled and squawked, but I was strengthened by my madness. I held her firm while I produced a tool and began clipping her feathers to prevent her escape. My confidence was soon betrayed: she was able to get her head loose and unleash a vicious bite, tearing deeply into the meat of my wrist.

Blinded by pain, I screamed and yanked my hand back. As I did, the shears savagely cut through her blood feathers. With my grasp loosened and her fury engendered, she burst free and, shrieking, fell to the ground, blood spraying the gray stones with every frenzied flap as she attempted to fly away.

I tore a strip of cloth from my shirt and bound it tightly to my wrist to stop the bleeding. When I looked down, the raven was gone – only a trail of blood glistening on the stone floor to show where she had dragged herself away. For the first time, I felt fear: it was too much blood for a bird.

I followed the trail, which continued around the parapet. When I reached the corner, I froze in my steps: The claw prints had changed to bare human footprints. I was afraid to turn the corner, but I summoned the courage and bolted into the unknown. There, lying on her side, was the most beautiful woman I had ever seen. She was naked, with alabaster skin that glistened with sweat in the moonlight, and waist-length, onyx-black hair.

She turned and screamed at me. It was a soul-wrenching cry of hurt and anguish. As she cradled her bleeding arm across her breasts, the blood tricked between them and down her stomach.

I slowly approached and cautiously knelt beside her. She frantically backed away, hissing at me, until, hitting the wall of the parapet and with no place to go, she resigned herself to her fate. I crawled to her on my knees, tearing more cloth to attempt to bandage the damage I had done. She fought me as I pulled her arm free and for the first time saw what my insanity had wrought – she was missing three fingers.

She took advantage of my stunned state and, in one motion, yanked her crippled limb from my grasp, unsteadily rose to her feet, staggered to the wall – and hurled herself off the parapet!

Madness! I impotently fumbled to try to grab her – which is when I saw her fall, stretch out her arms and change into the form of a raven – the raven

I had so heartlessly injured! She could only glide and not well; but it was sufficient to place herself at great distance from my shears. I watched as she awkwardly flew to the safety of another tower. I collapsed seated against the stone wall, gasping for breath, folding my legs to my chest and gripping them with my arms, rocking back and forth trying to hold on to my sanity.

Over the next few days, I searched for the injured raven woman. At times, I would see her fly from tower to tower. One morning, I found her in human form outside the tower room that was my home. She was waiting for me.

I made a motion to approach. I opened my mouth to utter a thousand meaningless apologies. She held up her hand to stop me – the beautiful, delicate hand I had so rudely raped – revealing a full array of fingers.

I stopped my story, crying. The man sympathetically offered a handkerchief. I shook my head, urging him away. "As you can plainly see," I said, sobbing, "I'm no prize. No woman has ever shown an interest in me. When I was a boy, I kept ravens in our rooftop roost. I spent every waking moment caring for them. Loving them. They were my entire life."

"My mother was not understanding. She ordered me to spend less time with the ravens and more time doing normal things boys did. I tried to be one of them – but I was merely one, alone, among them. I loathed every minute of it – and so did my companions. But I always had my birds to come home to. Until one day..."

"I found them all dead in their roost. I vividly recall my mother, bottle in hand, as she walked up behind me, drunkenly laughing as I cradled each one of my beloved birds in my arms. Kissing their cold, limp bodies one by one. They were my entire life."

"I felt hate well up in me, fueled by her laughter and her choked singing, 'Four and twenty blackbirds, baked in a pie – an' wasn't that a tasty gift to set before the queen?!'"

"When she passed out on the floor amidst the ruined bodies I had brought down from the roof, mouth agape in a roaring alcohol snore, in that black, gaping maw I saw my destiny. We had no family, no friends to come calling. The next morning, I left the remains of my past behind and came here to offer my service to the Tower and began my apprenticeship. When the lead raven master retired, I was offered the position. I have been here ever since."

I opened the stove and tossed another log in to stoke the fire. I rubbed my hands to warm myself. The man sat motionless; his face a blank, unreadable canvas. I continued my tale.

We stood in my room in the Tower. "Do you understand what you have done? Do you know who I am? You only live because I have watched you caring for us, with such love," the woman raven said.

"No...tell me...please."

She walked about my room, eyes closed, fingering the meager objects I possessed. Her eyes suddenly snapped open. It seemed as if twin daggers had thrust themselves into my eyes as she looked at me. "You hunger," she said. "Hunger can drive even the soundest mind mad – and at a price."

Her voice was like the sweetest music. Melodic. Sensual. I knew not what to do.

"I hungered once. But I desired power and was cursed for my lust." She turned to me and took my shaking my hand in hers. "As I said, boy, every hunger has its price." She placed my hand under a soft breast, letting me feel its tender weight. My heart pounded. My throat tightened. And then she reached down and cupped my bollocks through my loose trousers. As I groaned, she huskily whispered in my ear, "Is your purse prepared to render payment?"

Wide-eyed, I shook my head in agreement. Had she been the Devil, I would have agreed to give her my soul. As if hearing my silent, frenzied offer, she slyly smiled and whispered, "I accept."

I had never been with a woman. But after that night, I knew I wanted to always be with one – and only my raven woman. I also knew she would not stay with me. That she would find another lover – a better lover, a more handsome lover. These thoughts tore at me as she lay beside me sleeping. I rose without waking her and paced the halls wildly muttering to myself. I loved her! But did she love me? Could she love me? Why? Why would she? I would make her! Yes, that was the only answer. I would make her forever mine.

She started from sleep with a moan when I locked the iron cuff around her ankle. "It burns! In the name of the Mother, it burns!" Fortunately, my room was far removed from any others, so her cries went unheeded by any but me. She did not lie: I could see ugly burn marks and blisters raise where the iron touched her skin. She stood up on the bed, her naked flesh flushed with anger as she frantically yanked at the chain to no avail. "You foolish, stupid boy! Bind me with iron? I will have your soul for this!" she wailed

Watching her thus did not scare me – it engendered even greater lust. While she raved, I lunged at her, knocking her to the bed. I forced myself inside of her, her wild thrashing only increased my passion. With each pounding thrust, my mind screamed, "Love me! Love me!"

Finally spent, I rolled off of her. She lay there motionless, glaring at me. If she burned, if she was hurt, she made no utterance. I dressed and sat in my chair watching her. And still that fiery gaze was all she gave me.

This was our life for some time.

I never touched her after that day; but I would not release her, knowing that she would flee forever. I offered her food and drink; I made attempts to clean her wounds; but she silently refused and overture. I begged her; but her eyes were hard, refusing. As each day ended, she would speak the only words she would utter.

"Set me free."

"Tomorrow," I would lie, knowing that I could never live without her.

One morning, I returned from my duties to find the room empty. The sheets were soaked with blood – and my shears, which I had carelessly left within her reach, lying on the floor, the blades clogged with flesh and gore.

I was inconsolable – and terrified. Now it was I who refused nourishment and water. I would do anything to get her back; but my very soul twisted in fear. Who or what was the object of my desire? Desperate, I paid a visit to the old raven master. I told him the whole tale, knowing it could mean torture or death should he reveal my shame. Instead, he looked at me piteously. "Alas, son," he said sadly, "You have done a more terrible thing than you can ever imagine. For she is Morgan le Fay."

I balked. This was no Arthurian legend, but a real woman! "Boy," he said sternly, "You would not believe in le Fay, and yet you come to me believing that you captured a bird that turned into a woman with whom you had carnal relations?"

Closing my eyes, I nodded for him to continue. "Morgan le Fay has been many women," he said, "for good or for ill is her reputation. None can truly say which is the real enchantress. But she has chosen to guard the Tower – penance? True guardian of the realm? Her motivation, as always, is known only to her."

"You, boy, have brought great evil upon yourself – perhaps us all – with your ignorance and lust." He pointed a thin, jagged finger at me and hissed, "You must earn her forgiveness. You must make it right – at any cost."

I left the old man. He had answered my question, but had done nothing to help me. I had offended one of the most potent mages in history – mages! It all seemed unreal. As I wandered back to my lonely room, I thought about the first time I saw her in her nakedness, held her breast, felt the softness of her lips against mine. Forgiveness? Bah! I spat. I did not want forgiveness. I did not want to "make it right." I wanted her!

But how to bring her back? It had been more than a month since her savage escape. I had not seen her anywhere in the Tower's demesnes. I looked up and saw the ravens circling overhead – and in an instant, I knew what would make her come.

Later that night as the ravens roosted, I plucked them down one by one and, with tears in my eyes, wrung their necks.

Oh yes, she would come.

"And did she come?"

The words came as a harsh slap to the face of an unconscious man.

35

"I asked, 'And did she come?'"

I looked at the stranger. His face was still as placid as when I started my tale. It was then that I realized that I had come to the end of it. I knew what had to be done. I stood up and stared down at the tiny form swaddled on my bed. Yes. I knew what had to be done.

"Yes, sir," I continued, "she came. Last night, as I was walking the grounds, she appeared in human form in a billowing white dress, unaffected by the cold, unstained, undamaged – perfect. She clutched this very same bundle lying here tight to her chest. With little delicacy, she forced it into my hands. 'Look,' she commanded. 'Look and see what you have created – the only such act you have ever performed.' I opened the swaddling and set my eyes upon the most beautiful babe I had ever seen. 'You who have destroyed so much because you cared only for yourself must now care for something other than yourself.'"

"I dropped to my knees, holding the child, wailing like a babe myself, pleading with her for her forgiveness, her love, to remain with me. 'Love?' she laughed, 'What do you know of love? You know only desire – they are not the same. Well, boy, you are going to learn the difference.' She pointed at the baby. 'This will teach you the sacrifice that is love. When you are ready to give of yourself for the sake of another, only then will you have learned. And only then will I consider your plea.'"

"She stood over me as I bowed my head and wept. When I looked up again, she was gone. I took the infant back to my room, placed it on the bed and stared at it. I knew nothing of caring for another human being – all I had known was myself and my ravens. It started to cry and I instinctively picked it up and held it to my chest. It was then that I felt it start to squirm – beneath the swaddling, I could feel it…changing. A sharp, claw-like pain tore through my chest and I dropped the bundle to the bed. When I looked down, there was a bloody rend in my shirt and an ugly cut on my skin, as if from a…"

There lay the babe, her angelically beautiful face shining up at me. Hesitatingly, I reached down and with shaking hands opened up the blanket, praying that I would see the pink, cherubic form of a newborn. And then I saw the small wing covered with sleek, black downy feathers and heard the child…cry?"

I gathered the babe from my bed and handed her to the stranger. "You asked earlier if I needed your assistance and I refused. I was wrong. I have been wrong too much – and have wronged too much. But no more. Here. Take the child. She is yours." The stranger took the child into his arms and bowed his head, never once removing his gaze from me. "It is the right thing to do," he said.

The right thing. At last, I must do the right thing. "Please excuse me, sir," I said. "She calls and I must go to her."

The strange man with the foundling watched as his host left the comfort of the warm room and, without looking back, walked to the parapet. Nor did he attempt to move when he saw the man leap into the air, arms flung out at his sides and disappear into the night. After a moment, he slowly rose and deliberately donned his coat and hat before swaddling the child more closely against the winter chill. Together, they entered the night. The baby softly cooed and he pulled back the blanket to reveal a sweet smile – and he smiled back. Above, a raven cawed. The man tipped his hat and bowed. "Thank you for your trust, M'lady. It is an honor to serve you. I will raise her as my own."

He watched as the raven swooped down from its perch to the shattered body splayed on the flagstones below.

And feasted.

TENT 4

BARKING MAD
Jeffrey Stundel

"Chester Pettigrew, scribe and journalist!" the man said cheerily, grabbing the other man's hand, pumping it with wild enthusiasm. "I can't tell you – I simply can't tell you – what an absolute pleasure it is to meet you!" The other man looked down at their arms, leaping about like two cats fighting over a fish, and slowly raised his eyes to fix an unpleasant gaze on his counterpart. Chester Pettigrew rarely saw beyond his own nose, so the deadly stare was lost on him. He merely gushingly continued, "Yes, what an absolute pleasure it is to meet a man as famous as you! A legend! A reputation that precedes itself! My God, shaking the hand of the one and only Dr. Sarcoma!"

An almost imperceptible twitch danced across the corner of the man's mouth, barely breaking the placid plane of his face. It was impossible to know if it was a suppressed grin or scowl, for only his eyes seemed to speak as Pettigrew continued singing praises like a broken calliope. The man said nothing. He pulled out a pocket watch, clicked open the cover, took note of the time, closed the cover and proceeded to nonchalantly, but deliberately, wind up the mechanism while waiting for Pettigrew's to wind down.

"…words, words, words so what 'dark desire' will you be sharing with me with which I can thrill my readers?" Pettigrew said, finally getting to the point. "My readers hang on my every word (the man thought 'themselves' was missing from the statement) – 'The Bard of Belleville' they call me. Indeed! When I saw your wagons pass through town, I immediately said to myself, 'Chester – now there is a diversion worthy of old Will himself! By God, Caliban himself would be right at home among your tents! As Prospero said, 'Nature hath framed strange fellows in her time!'"

"*The Merchant of Venice*," muttered the man, "not *The Tempest*," as he started rubbing the skull on the end of his cane with his fingers. Had Pettigrew bothered to notice anything but himself, he would have seen how distinctly white the man's knuckles were, even whiter than his skin. "I'm sorry? Did you say something?" asked Pettigrew; but knowing that no one else had anything to say more valuable than him, he plowed on. "Yes, so 'some strange fellows,' to be sure. And that is why I am here…"

The man stopped Pettigrew as he opened his mouth to suck in the remaining air of the beautiful state of Virginia. "Mr. Pettigrew, thank you for your kind words," he said, taking off his hat with a small bow. "You certainly are a man of many. In fact, I hope that you will be so generous as to leave a few for me – for I am a man of few."

Pettigrew took this as a compliment and was preparing a profuse thanks, when the man took advantage of the rare pause. "No, no," he said sweetly, with arsenic-laced honey on his tongue, "Please. There is no need to thank me for the gift of your silence," he said, before looking behind himself and gritting through a toothy grin, "I guarantee it is one you can never return." Returning to face Pettigrew, he said with a more benevolent, but equally toothy, smile, "But I'm quite sure that you want to learn more about my humble 'diversion' before meeting Serpina, the Snake Lady."

Cutting Pettigrew off in mid inhalation, the man said, donning his hat and pointing the way with his cane, "Absolutely! Right this way, Mr. Pettigrew."

As they began their walk, the man whipped his cane up to (and with a wince-inducing smart, into) Pettigrew's chest, stopping him in his tracks. "Ah, one thing before we proceed," the man said, "please do remember to maintain the dignity of my family – you are our guest, not a patron. I ask that you remember that they are people: remain respectful. And, most of all," he added with a teacher's stare, pulling back the cane as Pettigrew rubbed his stinging pectorals, "do not speak unless spoken to."

The two men strolled the tented lanes, with the man sharing tidbits of the carnival's history, as well as brief biographies of, as he called them to Pettigrew's curiosity, family members. The reverence that they paid him was almost childlike, and he addressed them not as an owner, but as a father. "These freaks, they certainly do love you Dr. Sciatica!"

The man stopped as if frozen in place, while Pettigrew continued walking and talking, not noticing or seeming to care that he was speaking only to and for himself – he did this often, as he enjoyed being his own entertainment and audience. If teeth could crack under the strain of being gnashed, the man's would have shattered in his mouth. This was a bad day – a sad anniversary for him – and, perhaps, the only time his emotions found themselves surfacing. Which meant it was going to be a worse day for Chester Pettigrew. "No, there's already a body there," the man muttered hoarsely, closing his eyes, trying to regain his composure while fending off a coincidental hunger for a helping of boiled cow tongue – meanwhile, Pettigrew continued his oration to the air.

"nothing, nothing, nothing so, Dr. Cicada – do you mind if I call you 'Cicada'? Are you a real doctor, or is it just an honorary title?" It was then that

Pettigrew realized that he was a good twenty yards in front of his host. He walked back and found the man standing with his eyes tightly shut, moving his lips without saying a word.

"Ah, an afternoon prayer. So, you're a man of God, eh? I *am* impressed! My nephew wanted to be a priest; but my sister said, 'Johnny, you know you fall asleep in church.' Quite honestly, I…" The man's eyes snapped open and his lips stopped moving. His body relaxed. He looked at his watch again, nodded and smiled. Suddenly, he displayed a familiarity that took Pettigrew by surprise. The man put his arm in Pettigrew's and started walking, kicking out his long legs and letting his cane swing freely from front to back. "*Mr.* Pettigrew. I've changed my mind. I believe I have the *perfect* member of my family for you to meet. In fact," he added with that unnatural grin, "I'm quite certain you'll never be able to conduct another interview once you've met with him."

"Why, Dr. Siracusa, that is too kind of you!" Pettigrew gleefully chirped, grabbing the man's hand for round two of the catfight. "Mr. Pettigrew, please," the man scolded, extricating his hand, "You mustn't wear out your writing arm with these pleasantries – you are about to meet your profession's just reward and will need it to complete your assignment."

The man looked around and saw a carnival worker. Waving him over, he said, "Gregory, if you would. Please run ahead and ensure that Bartleby is not otherwise engaged – I have a special guest for him, Mr. Chester Pettigrew, journalist and 'bard'." Pettigrew beamed at the word "bard". Gregory grew pale at the name Bartleby. "Uh, Bartleby? But he…I mean, Dr. Sarcophagus – "

"No 'buts', Gregory," the man said, giving a knowing nod, "Yes, Bartleby. Now, run along."

"Oh!" cried Pettigrew, dramatically slapping himself on the forehead, "I am a dunce! I am so sorry, Dr. Saprophagous. How could I have so rudely mispronounced your name all of this time? You, sir, are a true gentleman for not correcting me!"

Dr. Sarcophagus shook his head. "Do not worry about it." Putting his arm around Pettigrew's shoulder and, walking him to a sparsely tented section of the carnival, laughed, "That is the least of your problems!" Pettigrew released a guffaw without truly understanding what it was he was laughing at.

Arriving at a lone tent, set some hundred yards from the carnival, Dr. Sarcophagus explained, "Bartleby prefers his privacy, so we respect his wishes. He is one of the carnival's oldest family members, but he no longer performs. He is – well, sensitive. And he doesn't do well with the crowds. He takes them a bit too…well, when you meet him, you will understand."

Dr. Sarcophagus opened the canvas flap that served as a door and stuck his head inside. "Bartleby? I have a visitor for you," he called. A gruff, accented voice called from the darkness, "Yeah. Greg told me. And I told him he could take Mr. Visitor and…" Dr. Sarcophagus pulled his head out and said to Pettigrew with a smile, "Would you wait here just one moment?" and entered the tent. Some words that Pettigrew couldn't make out were exchanged – some heated, some calming. When the doctor reappeared, he smiled and beckoned Pettigrew to enter.

"Mr. Pettigrew," Dr. Sarcophagus said, shaking the journalist's hand, "I can't tell you that it's been a pleasure spending this afternoon with you. But you must excuse me; it is a show night and I am needed at the carnival." He turned away, but turned back to Pettigrew as if remembering something and said, "Bartleby will be showing you the way out."

And walked away, letting loose a laugh that Pettigrew thought would blow down the tents.

Well, thought Pettigrew, fortune favors the brave, and walked into the tent.

The first thing that struck Pettigrew was the overwhelming scent of old, cheap cigars. Everything reeked of the aroma. He held his handkerchief over his face trying not to cough or sneeze. The lights were low, but Pettigrew could see the figure of an extremely large man sitting in an easy chair, his face lit by the glowing embers of a cigar with each sizzling puff. In those brief moments of illumination, Pettigrew was struck by how full the man's beard was – it seemed to reach high on his cheeks almost to his eyes.

Suddenly, a voice pierced the half-shadows. "Well, ya ain't got that long. You gonna sit down, or what?"

Pettigrew asked, "Good sir, would it be too much trouble for a bit more light? It will make it easier for me to write."

"Suit yerself," was the reply. Pettigrew could hear the hiss of gas as the lamp began to glow more brightly. It was a good thing he still had the handkerchief over his mouth, or he would have screamed. Instead, he stood there staring in disbelief.

The golden eyes turned into glowing slits, reflecting the burning cigar. "Ya lookin' at somethin', boy?" came a growl.

It was a man. No, it was a large dog. No, dogs don't smoke cigars, drink beer and wear bib overalls. Yes, that's what it was, Pettigrew thought panic stricken, it was a man dressed as a dog.

"Ya some kind of a priss? What's with th' snotrag?" the – man – said, blowing out a puff of smoke the size of the emission of a steam train. Realization struck him and he pulled the cigar out from between his – holy Mother of God, look at those teeth! – looked at it thoughtfully, then at Pettigrew, and heartily laughed, "Oh, ya don't like my stogies! Well, pal, fer th' next however long yer here, ya better get to like 'em!"

Pettigrew stuttered, "Uh – uh – may – may I sit down?" The man put waved the cigar around exasperated and yelled, "Why th' Hell did I ask ya to sit down if I didn't want ya to sit down?! You an idiot, boy? If yer auditionin', don't bother – we already got one." He put the cigar back in his mouth, placed his hands behind his head and crossed his leg, saying nothing.

The journalist quickly sat down and began fidgeting on his lap with his pen and notebook, equally silent and terrified as to what to do or say.

"BOO!"

It wasn't a word, it was a roar that filled the entire tent and made the canvas wave. Pettigrew almost jumped out of his clothes and ran home naked. His host leaned back and roared again – this time with laughter.

"Bwahahaha! Oh, mother! You shoulda seen yer face, boy!" He was holding his sides, bent over at the waist. "Oh, that was rich. Didn't go messin' yer pants, didja boy? Yer cleanin' the seat cushion if ya did!"

Pettigrew, his ego pierced through from front to back, forgot his fear. "That, sir, was uncalled for! I am a professional!" he reprimanded. The man only laughed harder, because when Pettigrew stood up to deliver his remonstrance, a wet spot was clearly evident on the front of his pants.

"AAAAHHHHAHAHAHA! Ya – ya *peed* yerself?! Oh, man! An' here I thought this was goin' to be a waste o' time. Stop it! Stop it! Yer killin' me...ohhhh, oohhh, ooooohh!" the man started panting as he gasped for air in between laughs.

Pettigrew had had enough. He was not going to be insulted by a...a freak! He launched into his typical response when insulted – using Elizabethan words to prove his intellectual, if not physical, superiority.

It was a mistake.

"You will stop your laughter this instant! You, sir, are an insolent cur!"

The man choked off his laughter and spat his cigar on the floor. Uncrossing his leg and gripping the arms of the chair, he slowly stood up. His bulk seemed to fill the entire half of the tent he occupied.

"What...did...ya...call...me?"

Pettigrew fumbled, "I, uh, er, I..."

The man was on him in what seemed to be one stride. He grabbed Pettigrew by his tie and collar, lifted him up and snarled in his face, "WHAT DID YA CALL ME?!?!" The wetness of spit on Pettigrew's face made him forget the new wetness in the back of his pants. He babbled and cried an endless stream of apologies and entreaties.

This was no man. This was a beast.

The thing rudely hurled him back into his chair like a toy doll. "Goddammit!" he screamed, "I had enough o' that shit when I was out front o' this carnival! Ya don't come in here an' call me that! Where th' Hell is Sarcophagus?!"

It stormed around the tent picking up and throwing things. Pettigrew sat in his waste praying that he would be forgotten. "An' YOU!" No, he wasn't. A finger (claw?) was pointed at his nose, as he was once again hoisted in the air by the collar. "Remind me again: why th' Hell are ya here? An' make it short, or I'll stick yer head so fer up yer ass you'll be burpin' farts!"

Somehow, Pettigrew could get out, "I – I – I am Chester Pettigrew, journalist with *The Belleville Bulletin*. I came to write a story about the carnival for the newspaper."

The man seemed to relax a bit and lowered Pettigrew down until his feet were again touching the floor. He stepped back and took a long look at Pettigrew. "Newspaper, huh?" He looked at Pettigrew's pen and pad on the floor, and walked away, mumbling to himself. Pettigrew had a chance to look at his host, too. He didn't look like a man in a dog suit at all. He looked like a man-sized dog, his features a mélange of both.

Pettigrew picked up his pen and notebook, and, his journalistic curiosity kicking in, sat down – albeit gingerly thanks to the soft, extra padding in his pants. He cleared his throat and asked as calmly as he could, "So, sir, what may I ask is your name?" The man went to a table and opened a box of cigars. He bit off the tip and lit the other end with a wooden match.

Through a billow of smoke, he said, "Bartleby. They used to call me 'Th' Dog-Faced Boy.'"

"Ah," said Pettigrew brightly, "Like Melville's character! Bartleby the Scrivener! 'I'm sorry sir, but I would prefer not to.' Wonderful story about the futility of our day-to-day existence. Personally, every day for me is an adventure. Take today for instance, why…"

Bartleby held up a meaty hand/paw. "Boy, I don't know what yer talkin' about an' I don't care. I'm guessin' ya want to learn 'bout me. I don't mind tellin', 'specially if Dr. S. wants me to. But yer gonna play by my rules: shut yer piehole an' listen. Got it?"

Pettigrew was already in his old mode, so he launched into, "Why, certainly, sir – I know what that can be like: people talking and not listening. It is so rude and I get so impatient sometimes that I –"

Bartleby popped the metal cap off of a bottle of beer, took a long swig that emptied the bottle and said, "Okay. I see this is gonna be harder than I thought. So, we're gonna make a deal, 'kay? Ya get three – no, five – chances to piss me off. After th' fifth chip's cashed, I rip yer friggin' head off. Sound good?"

Pettigrew had quickly grown accustomed to his host's gruffness and took this as a sign of good humor on his part. He decided to join in the fun. "Absolutely! I'm not usually a gambling man, but this is your house and your rules. The last time I played a game of chance was in New Orleans – like I said, I'm not much of a gambler and –"

The man sat down heavily in his chair and rubbed his face. "Okay. That one I'll give ya fer free. Th' next one's gonna cost ya."

"So," said Pettigrew, ignoring the warning, "Let's begin at, well, the beginning! Where were you born?"

"A little flyspeck of a town in central Florida that ya never heard of. Next question."

Oh, thought Pettigrew, he was going to be *that* kind of a subject. Well, not a problem – he'd dealt with people like this before. He had the gift of making anyone feel comfortable with opening up to him.

"How old are you?"

"Old enough," he answered, cracking open and downing another beer with growing frustration. "Now, are ya gonna ask me what ya really want to, or are we just gonna dick around?"

"Very well, sir," said Pettigrew, "If you wish, we can dispense with the chit chat and get down to business." Taking a deep breath, he ventured, "So, how did you come to be the Dog-Faced Boy?"

Bartleby struck his earlier pose of repose, blowing smoke into the already polluted air. "Well," he replied with a smile through his teeth-clenched cigar, "I wasn't born this handsome, that's fer damn sure."

"I was as normal as," he giggled, "you, until I was about thirteen or thereabouts. Then I started *changin'*. Scared th' livin' bejeesus outta my folks, th' first time they came to help me with my prayers an' found me in my pajamas lookin' like this."

"They was a god-fearin' couple an' thought I was damned or somethin'. Took me that night to th' preacher. He slapped me 'round pretty good tryin' to beat th' devil outta me. Thing is, he got more of th' devil than he 'spected. He never did use his cross-bearin' arm again – nothin' much left of it."

"Thing is, that once I got it outta my system, well, I was back to bein' me again. Never could figure out what started it the first time. But after that, well, damn, ya didn't never want to get me riled up! Funny thing is that folks always felt kinda funny 'round me. Dogs, though, they loved me – even th' ones everyone said was needin' to be put down."

"At first, I didn't let myself get angry. But everyone who knew 'bout what had happened either feared or laughed at me. That's when they all started callin' me 'Dog Face'. I can tell ya, it only took one or two times of that shit for me to take off th' gloves an' show 'em I wasn't nobody's dog."

Bartleby trailed off. It seemed like he was genuinely sad thinking about his younger days. Pettigrew, of course, saw his dramatic pause as an opportunity to talk.

"So, you got angry and took on the appearance of a dog," he said almost jokingly. Although the living evidence was before him, he still found it hard to believe. He couldn't resist himself from asking, "Did you take on any of the characteristics of a dog? Did you, for instance, find yourself preferring trees to toilets?" Ah, Pettigrew. You are so witty, he thought.

Something stung his forehead – he reached up and felt a bloody cut. In his lap was a beer bottle cap. Pettigrew angrily looked across at Bartleby; but before he could speak, Bartleby cut him off. "Chip one, chump. Four more to go."

Gingerly dabbing at the wound with his handkerchief, Pettigrew asked petulantly, "Are you going to throw anything else at me?" Bartleby waved off his complaint. "Are ya going to ask me any more smart-ass questions, smart ass?"

Pettigrew said nothing. He was here and he was a professional – he *would* complete this interview for the sake of his readers!

Forging ahead, he asked, "Well, it would appear that, at first, you only became a dog when angered. Why is it that you are still in the form?"

Bartleby smiled an evil, toothy grin. "I dunno, genius. Could it be 'cause I'm angry *all th' friggin' time*?! Live my life an' see if y'ain't permanently pissed. My folks abandoned me after 'bout a year o' this an' I had to fend fer myself. Try bein' 14 or 15 years old, never bein' on yer own an' havin' to figure it all out fer yerself – not just livin', but *life*! Alone, they're a bitch – try 'em together when yer nuthin' but a kid!"

He got up and started pacing – often coming uncomfortably close to Pettigrew, who would draw back from him. "See!" yelled Bartleby, throwing up his arms, "That's what I'm talkin' 'bout! Ya think I'm gonna hurt ya? I dunno, maybe eat ya? Jeesus friggin' Christ on a tractor all I'm doin' is walkin' by ya! Here, I got 'nother one fer ya. Try gettin' laid lookin' like this! Can't get near a woman, 'less I pay 'er – an' even that's a dicey proposition."

Pettigrew muttered, "I guess not everyone likes it 'doggy style'."

Bartleby whirled on his heel. "What was that, shithead?" he said with a steely, smoldering stare. "I think I missed that – oh, I know," he said, affecting a snobby, British accent, "Pip, pip! But I do believe I need another reminder of our bet!" Suddenly, quick as a flash, another bottle cap hit Pettigrew in the forehead, this time embedding itself about an eighth of an inch in his skin. As he painfully peeled it out, Bartleby strode back to his chair, flinging himself into it with a thud that sent vibrations through the dirt floor. "Two down, Hemingway, three to go."

With a loud pop, Bartleby opened another beer and gained another projectile. He took a gulp and said, "But I'll answer yer question a bit better. See how I am? This is ain't th' full deal. I ain't this way all th' time – then," he added with a wicked playfulness, "I'm a Hell of a lot more fun."

"But," he continued, "this is how I was when Dr. S. found me – or, really, I found him. Before that, I knocked 'round a bit. Went from town to town, tryin' to stay out of people's way an' keepin' them out of mine. Animals – now, they're my friends. Well, not all animals. Cats – bitchy, whiny, know-it-all twats," he said downing his beer, adding with a snicker, "they remind me o' – newspaper writers."

"So, yeah. Every town, I always found work as th' dogcatcher – like I said, never met a dog I didn't like or didn't like me. Things'd be good for a while – I'd stay 'normal' an' not get into any tussles. But, then, some asshole would get wind from a buddy who knew a guy who heard 'bout someone who met me like this – an' it'd be like one of them gunslingers in the West. Everyone wanted to 'see th' beast' fer himself an' test me out."

"I gotta tell ya," Bartleby said darkly, "ain't *no one* seein' th' beast an' livin' to tell 'bout it. So, I'd either get run outta town or take off 'fore anyone started takin' 'fense at missin' an arm – or a family member."

"You mentioned Dr. Salmonella – tell me, how did you meet him?" Pettigrew inquired. "He seems like quite an interesting fellow – needs to brush up on his Shakespeare, though. We had a delightful time this afternoon, even though he tends to be a bit loquacious for my tastes. I was very impressed with how he feels about all of the freaks in the carnival, and –"

Pettigrew never saw the bottle until he came to.

"Feelin' better now, Sparky?" Bartleby was still in his chair, smoking another cigar. Pettigrew found himself lying on the floor with a headache the size of the Chesapeake. An empty beer bottle lay near his head. Unsteadily, he pushed himself up with his arms and sat on the floor trying to get his bearings. Through the haze of waking, Bartleby seemed distinctly – larger? Hairier? It was hard for Pettigrew to tell with the pounding in his head as a constant distraction.

Bartleby leaned over and pointed a finger in Pettigrew's direction and said, "Chip number three. An' don't you ever, *ever*, call any of us freaks again. If I hadn't made that deal with ya, yer head wouldn't be hurtin' – it'd be *missin'*. We're not th' freaks. *Yer* th' freaks – 'cause only freaks get pleasure outta seein' other people's pain. O' course," he said grinning, "I'm kinda likin' watchin' you right now, so what does that make me?"

Pettigrew finally righted himself, staggered to his feet and oozed into his chair. He lazily picked up his pen and notepad as Bartleby started speaking again, his handwriting an unreadable scrawl.

"Dr. S.? Well, he's th' best damn thing that ever happened to a guy like me. Hell, he's th' best thing that ever happened to every last – *person* – livin' here. He ain't our boss; he's our father. We don't ask questions 'bout him, just like we don't ask each other questions 'bout each other. That's th' rule here – ya speak when yer spoken to." Arching forward he added nastily, "An' I can tell ya that *you* wouldn't last an hour livin' with us."

"But, yeah, I was getting' the torches and pitchforks treatment when I run into th' carnival – literally. It was dark an' I was runnin' as fast as I could from a mob screamin' for my blood. I was humpin' this honey in her daddy's barn when Daddy came bustin' in – th' way she was howlin' you'd think she was, well, anyways, like I was sayin', in comes Daddy an' he takes a shot at me. With a gun, not his fist. He winged me good – an' th' change comes fast an' furious. Never stood a chance – either of 'em."

"Next mornin', someone sees me runnin' buck naked down th' road from th' farm an' hears Mama screamin' her head off. 'fore ya know it, there's a posse huntin' me down. They almost got me – plugged me a few times; but th' change saved me. After that, I never went back to how I was, always like this. Well, like I said 'fore, not *always*."

"Come night, I'm runnin' an' runnin' an' it's pitch black an' I'm freezin' my ass off. I run through a clump o' trees – an smack dab into a wagon. Dr. S.' wagon. He comes out dressed like ya seen him – never seen him dressed any different – an' starts talkin' to me like he was 'specting me or somethin'. He brings me into his tent, set up behind th' wagon, an' without askin' me who I am or why I'm runnin' 'round bare assed, gets some guy to bring me clothes an' food. First hot meal I'd had in days – never tasted nothin' so good."

Pettigrew, almost terrified to say anything, tried to come up with the most innocuous thing he could to add to the conversation. "That must have been a treat for you."

Flecks of red speckled Bartleby's golden eyes. Oh no, thought Pettigrew. He tried to dodge, but he was too slow. Another bottle cap dug into his forehead. "Bottom o' th' ninth, bases empty, two outs fer Chester Fuckstick. Know what, Chester? I'm thinkin' y'ain't gonna make it to th' end of my story!"

"Please," Pettigrew weakly begged, "No more."

"Hey," said Bartleby shrugging, "don't blame me; ain't my fault. If you'd keep yer mouth shut, 'stead of wearin' out yer gums..." Blowing off the suds from a fresh beer, he said blandly, "Well, it's yer move."

Pettigrew slumped in his chair. He was exhausted. Defeated. All he wanted to do was go home. Forget his promise to his readers. Journalistic integrity be damned. Peeking in through the top of the tent, the full moon shone down on the two men like a spotlight. The effect was not lost on the Bard of Belleville, who realized that he wasn't in a Shakespearean production – he was center stage for a bear baiting.

Standing up, Pettigrew, covered in filth, both his own and from the dirt floor, tried not to cry. He was drained of strength, of pride, of words. Swallowing hard and weak kneed, he steadied himself with the chair and said, shakily, "I think I must be going. I believe that I have taken up too much of your time. I thank you for this insightful afternoon and for your delightful candor. Please excuse me, I will be taking your leave now Barkleby."

Dr. Sarcophagus was admiring the same full moon while standing at the carnival entrance. Above the din, he could discern carnal howls and agonized screams. He shook his head.

People always forget, he thought, that dogs descended from wolves.

With a satisfied smile, Dr. Sarcophagus walked into the throng saying to no one in particular, "Goodnight, sweet prince. And flights of angels sing thee to thy rest."

TENT 5

THE DEVIL AND DR. SARCOPHAGUS
M.J. Hyman

Joey Sharpes began to feel like the eight ball was mocking him. For twenty minutes, the cue ball had chased it around the stained, dilapidated pool table like a horny rabbit looking for a hot date. Taking a deep breath, he pulled back his stick, closed one eye and then…

"I'm tellin' the truth! It was the Devil himself, sure as I'm standin' here!"

The sudden outburst from an all-too-familiar voice startled Joey. The one really had nothing to do with the other, since Joey was the worst pool player around – but his felt-scraping miss was the final straw. The crowd at Club Elite – what passed for a speakeasy in these parts of the Pine Barrens – went wild, raining a cacophony of jeers on Joey's ten-dollar bet of a parade.

Holding the pool cue tightly in his callused, working-man's hand, he approached the cause of his loss, Smithville's resident reprobate, Ned "Red" Leeds. "That tears the drawers off a whore!" Joey roared as he charged at Leeds. "I'm gonna take my ten bucks outta yer drunk ass, ya loudmouthed rummy!"

Leeds had been trying to sucker drinks from a group of Atlantic City hotel workers with tall tales of the Barrens when all Hell broke lose. He abandoned his quest for libation and ran to the nearest corner, where he cowered in anticipation of Joey's attack. Red covered his head with his hands and pathetically pleaded, "Not in the face! Please Joey, not in the face!"

Joey grinned and acidly replied, "Glad ya said that. Now I know *exactly* where to put this piece of oak…" Joey raised the cue high over his head and began to bring it down with a speeding whistle that split the tobacco smoke-filled air. All Red could do was close his eyes and flinch.

Just as he was making his final prayers to his maker, Red heard a cracking that reminded him of a pine tree snapping in a winter ice storm. He opened one eye to look, when he realized that it wasn't a cue on his head that created the sound. Red's eyes were fixed on Joey's cue stopped six inches from its mark by an intervening walking stick. He followed his salvation from its silver tip and then to the tall, thin man in the top hat who seemed to be effortlessly holding Joey at bay.

Red also saw that Joey and "Top Hat" were locking eyes as well as sticks with one another. While Joey looked startled and apprehensive, the older gent's face was a picture of serenity.

"Tut, tut, dear sir," said the tall man to the still unmoving Joey. "There's no need for violence. I'll gladly pay you the sum you so richly deserve and..." then lowering his stick and grandly sweeping it in the direction of the now quietly staring crowd, "...I'll buy a round of this fine establishment's best whiskey for the entire house." The tall man then placed his hand on Joey's shoulder, which broke the spell on him.

Joey looked around at the faces. Some were as startled as he – others bore the unmistakable hint of whispers and snickers at his expense. He knew he was beaten – and didn't want to risk total embarrassment. He uttered a quick, "Yeah, sure. That'll be swell. Yeah, that's just fine...I gotta get home anyway an' see what the missus is up to." The richly dressed man reached into his coat pocket, produced a gold coin and pressed it into Joey's hand. The coin was quickly pocketed without even a look as to its authenticity as Joey mechanically walked out of the speakeasy and into the summer night.

While Joey Sharpes weaved his way home, the bartender took his finger off of the trigger of the shotgun hidden under the bar and began filling the stranger's request for free drinks for the patrons. The tall man had slapped on the bar another gold coin similar to the one he had given Joey. The man flinchingly accepted the "Thanks, pal!" and slaps on the back from the bar patrons and handed them all flyers to attend something called "The Carnival of Dark Desires" that had set up shop outside of town.

Eventually, they were too deep in their glasses to think about their benefactor, allowing him to sidle over to Red, who had ensconced himself at a table in the corner. When handed a flyer, Red waved it a way with a gesture that he wanted his free drink, too. "Don't think me an ingrate, as ya saved me from a good shellacking; but I really could use one o' the drinks ya gave to the other Pineys."

The man sitting opposite him shook his head, smiling like a wolf at a sheep wearing a wreath of mint and replied, "Dear, oh, dear! Where are my manners?" Like a vaudevillian magician, he flourished his empty sleeves – and magically a silver engraved flask appeared on the table. "Please," he intoned in a quiet, measured voice, "imbibe." He then added, "As the great Bard's Puck said:

"If we shadows have offended, Think but this, and all is mended, That you have but slumber'd here, While these visions did appear. And this weak and idle theme, No more yielding but a dream, Gentles, do not reprehend: if you pardon, we will mend: And, as I am an honest Puck, If we have unearned luck, Now to 'scape the serpent's tongue, We will

make amends ere long; Else the Puck a liar call; So, good night unto you all. Give me your hands, if we be friends. And Robin shall restore amends."

Red, feeling like he was drifting on a cloud in a dream, moved his lips in sync with the words – where had he heard them before? And did he care, as he took a long pull from the stranger's flask? His eyes widened like an owl's when the liquor hit his tongue. He was awash in sensation – memories, pouring over him like a luxurious, warm waterfall. Red then closed his eyes and thought of the words…he remembered them. *"Midsummer Night's Dream.* Haven't thought 'bout that play since I was in school." He sat there as the fluid filled every vein, relaxing his mind and body.

After a time, he opened his eyes and sighed. "Whoowee. Where'd ya get that stuff? That ain't the kinda coffin varnish we get from the bootlegs here'bouts." The man picked up the flask and, with a surreptitious wipe of the lip with a cloth, brought it to his lips for a deep draught. A twinkle seemed to travel from one eye to the other – or so Red thought. "You know fine literature and beverages, good sir. Please," he said, proffering the flask again, "have another sip."

The man slyly watched as Red drank. "This fine liqueur is from the private cellar of a now-deceased tsar. It was given to me by his family's…er…'caretaker' when we had chance to meet on the shores of the Baltic Sea. A religious fellow whom history will say was a madman. But to me, he will always be a greater escape artist than Houdini."

Red went to take another pull, but the man gently reached for the flask and took it away. Before Red could violently protest, the man tsked, "Now, now. When I walked in earlier I sat in a corner and heard you telling a most fascinating story before you almost lost…your good looks to that other fellow – who, I might add, left with my gold in his pocket. Don't you think you owe me the rest of the story before we," he said as he lifted up the flask and shook it from side to side, "continue our journey into the Romanoff's legacy here?"

Red, smiled back. He winked at the tall man and said "Of course. But we ain't been properly introduced. "My name is Ned Leeds, but everyone around here calls me…"

The top hatted man finished his sentence, "'Red'. Am I correct?"

"Yep. That's the ticket. Now, what's yer name, pal?"

"I'm Dr. Sarcophagus. An ancient name that means…"

"'Flesh eater'," said Red, now finishing the other man's sentence.

Dr. Sarcophagus' eyes flashed wider. "Yes. Exactly."

He furrowed his brow and seemed to be looking into Red's very soul. "This is most fascinating. You know Shakespeare and you understand Latin. I assume you were not always the inebriated wastrel you appear to be. Pray," he said, tipping a white-gloved hand in Red's direction, "edify me further as to how you wound up this way, Mr. Leeds. I am an observer of the human condition, and you intrigue one as 'well read' as me."

At first, Leeds' face was full of satisfaction with his companion's praise; but then he squinted and started rubbing his temples as if trying to awaken a long-sleeping genie in its bottle.

He sighed and said, "Look. First thing ya gotta know is that my family has been in these parts since there was 'these parts'. We even got a shit-spit o' land named after us not far from here. My dad died in the Spanish Flu epidemic an' I had to leave school to work in the pig iron mills. I hated every ball bustin' minute of it an' was glad when the mill closed. My mom died soon after an' I went to look for work in Atlantic City. Always a good swimmer, I worked like Judas' lawyer until I finally qualified as a lifeguard in Atlantic City an' then went to school in the evenin', got my diploma an' applied for an' became a county constable."

Dr. Sarcophagus picked up the flask and offered it again to Leeds. The man gratefully accepted and drank again. Wiping his mouth with the back of his filthy hand he went further into his story.

"I eventually worked my way up to chief officer of Atlantic County." A twisted, bemused smirk formed on his lips. It stopped when Leeds tipped his head back and guffawed. A few heads turned in his direction, but soon went back to their alcoholic debauches sneering at the "rummy".

Leeds sneered back as he grandly waved his arm around the room. "Hah! Back then, I was the one throwin' bums like me into the can an' keepin' law an' order in this fuckin' lunatic asylum." He grew quiet as his humor slowly devolved into somber reflection and sad regret.

Sensing that his drinking partner was about to descend into weeping self-recrimination, Dr. Sarcophagus pursed his lips and quickly said, "So, how does a cop become a criminal?"

"It was the Devil," Leeds muttered.

Dr. Sarcophagus' eyebrows lifted in surprise. "The Devil?" he half-chuckled. "Now, I have a great knowledge of 'Old Scratch' – actually, much better than most. But usually he…"

"Not that Devil, ya fancified dope!" Leeds shouted, his anger burning through the gray clouds of reflection. "I mean the JERSEY DEVIL. Ever hear of it?" he fumed, banging his hands on the table, making everything bounce. Shouts of "Knock it off!" and "Christ! Not that again!" rang out from the collected patrons.

"You mean the old legend of the bastardly conceived child of a supposed witch who lived in these parts centuries ago? I thought it was a…" replied Sarcophagus, his voice trailing off and reappearing in amusement, "…myth." Leeds' police skills were mostly dormant, but he could still sniff out bullshit – and recognize mockery. "Ya think I'm a loon – just like the others?!" he said, raising his voice above the din of the crowd. "Why? 'cause I'm a drunk?!

Yeah, I'm a drunk, Mr. Fancypants – but that don't make me crazy!" he wailed.

A voice from a few tables away came with a laugh, "It ain't 'cause yer crazy – it's 'cause yer an asshole!" That was followed by another celebrant's, "AN' a drunk!"

The place devolved into a sea of derision, all sending its waves washing over the chagrined Leeds. Snarling, he got up to face the crowd, prepared to take them all on. Dr. Sarcophagus reached up and gently, but firmly, tugged at his sleeve while ordering another round for the jeering Pineys. The coating of alcohol soothed the troubled waters.

"Laugh all ya want, ya hyenas," Leeds muttered to no one as he sat down, hands clenched on the table, head bowed. He sat there quietly for a few moments, and Sarcophagus was beginning to think that he had lost his narrator. Then a whispered voice started to quiver. "It was seven years ago this very night that the Devil went on his rampage."

"Y'know, I wasn't always a drunken sot," Leeds said with genuine sadness in his voice. "I was a sober man who'd never touched a drop before all that…shit happened." He lifted his weary, red-rimmed eyes to Dr. Sarcophagus without lifting his head and sighed, barely audibly, "I'd give anythin' to be the man I was."

Dr. Sarcophagus placed a hand on Leeds' shoulder, as if trying to impart strength to a lost soul. He said sympathetically, while gripping Leeds and giving him a convincing shake, "Ned, I think I can be of service to you. But I need to hear the rest of what happened." Whether it was the encouraging touch or the perceptible softening in the doctor's own eyes, Leeds relaxed. He came out of his slouch, stretched and heaved a huge sigh – and then began his story with a cautioning preface. "I'll tell ya all 'bout it, Doc. But I'm warnin' ya – the name of that thing is only half as horrible as seein' it. An' seen it I have!"

Leeds reached for the flask for another shot of Dutch courage – but as he brought it to his opening lips he stopped and stared at it. With a look of disgust, he gave a negative shake of his head, screwed the cap back on and forcefully handed the flask back to Dr. Sarcophagus with an expression of what amounted to triumph.

Okay Doc, here's where it all started…

After the mills an' factories shut down across the area after the war, prohibition began. The locals, lookin' for work an' not findin' any, wound up gettin' into bootleggin', prostitution an' anythin' else that would feed a starvin' family. Sometimes ya gotta do what ya gotta do. I had my hands full tryin' to keep all of it under control. As I told ya, I was tryin' to be the law an' order that the Barrens had never had. It was my county an' my people, an' I was duty bound to protect 'em. Mostly from themselves.

Sure, I had a few deputy constables; but they was all fellow Pineys. They had relatives or friends to protect, an' soon I couldn't rely on anyone but myself. The state ignored when I asked for help. I kept on 'em, an' when I finally did hear, they said that the area had such a small population that it didn't need more'n myself to keep order.

Well, that was it. All the way up the chain, people was gettin' paid off to keep the flow o' hooch goin'. Gangsters like Al Capone an' the rest had become public heroes an' strutted around like cocks o' the walk – never tried to hide what they was doin'. An' what they was doin' was makin' a boatload o' dough from the gamblin' an' whorehouses. Crime in the Barrens had become too goddamn profitable, an' no one was gonna help some "hick cop" interfere. "Fuck 'em!" I thought. If I was gonna be the only law around here, then that's what I was gonna be.

So, there I was sittin' alone in my little office just off the main street here in town. I had splittin' headache from the heat wave. Between that an' four people goin' blind that week from a bad batch o' moonshine, it was gettin' to be a bad summer for the Barrens.

An' it was 'bout to get worse.

All week I was gettin' calls an' visits from the outer area locals regardin' missin' animals an' damage done to their out buildin's. Barns, coops, kennels an' the like was havin' everythin' torn off 'em, includin' the paint. The buildin's wasn't the only things gettin' torn up: th' animals, from cows to bull pups, was bein' torn limb from limb. It was all I could to keep my dinner down from what I seen when I went out to investigate. I couldn't find a clue. No footprints, no other animal tracks, no blood trails…just no nothin', but the carcasses providin' a feast for the flies.

We'd had coyotes around here years before, but they was hunted an' chased all the way to the Ohio Valley an' not seen since. But the Barrens are a strange place, an' anythin' from those coyotes to a poacher, a hungry vagrant or who knows what could've done it. All I know is that I had to find out, or soon it would be my tired ass bein' torn apart an' lynched by the local Pineys. Livestock was precious durin' those times an' a man with a starvin' family ain't to be reasoned with when the cow providin' meat an' milk to his kids is spread out like a doormat to hunger.

I was fillin' out a report 'bout how a chicken farmer had lost all of his hens the night before. I was hopin' it was done by a pack o' rats or a weasel who had some whelps she was feedin', an' I planned to take a look later that day when the heat abated. I had just signed my name to the report when I heard the sound of an auto squealin' its tires an' racin' its motor as if it was parkin' at my door.

I ran outside an' saw Barney Morrison flyin' his jitney bus around the town square an' yellin' his head off out the car's window.

"It's back! For the love o' Jesus, it's back! The Devil's in the Barrens!" was what he kept screamin' over an' over. Barney musta seen me on the sidewalk an' started headin' his bus straight at me – an' he didn't look like he was gonna stop.

I was right.

I was barely able to get outta the way as the bus went right into a light pole not five feet from where I was standin'. The pole bent right over an' came crashin' down on its roof. I got to my feet an' ran over to see how bad things was.

It was pure chaos. People was runnin' outta stores all over the square. Some was screamin' for help; but no one was screamin' louder than Barney. I got to the bus an' saw that Barney was pinned behind the wheel an' the bus was fumin' like it might take flame any second. I yelled to the crowd for a couple of 'em to get a doctor an' run to the fire department just in case the bus caught went – or blew – up.

The whole time, even pinned down, Barney was still yellin' "The Devil! The Devil!" I reached in the window to try an' calm him down an' figure a way to get him free. Just then he looked over at me an' did somethin' amazin': With the strength of a madman he forced the wheel up enough to get offa him, an' then tumbled outta the broken door o' the bus.

Somehow he had escaped injury an' was now tryin' to stand up. He grabbed me by my shirt front, an' with eyes lookin' like they was gonna pop outta his head, yelled, "Holy mother o' mercy, Red! Thank God it's you! It almost got me! It ate Betty Donnen! In one bite! Ate her whole in one bite! Ohhh shit, I'm…"

An' then he passed out right there on the ground. I yelled for a couple o' the boys watchin' all this to help me get him to my office while we waited for the doc.

The doc came an' looked Barney over. He said it was a miracle he wasn't hurt worse. He laughed an' said that Barney was a tough old Irishman, an' outside of a couple o' cuts an' a bruised rib, he would be fine. He also told me that he was sober as a judge, an' now I really wondered what the Hell was goin' on.

The fire chief came in as the doc left. The chief was an old friend from my Atlantic City days an' said that the bus was a wreck, an' that he'd have his guys tow it away to a side alley. So here I was with a splittin' heat headache, almost run over by a bus an' stuck with a barely sane Piney who I had to try an' get sense out of. Like I said, I didn't drink back then – but that was gonna change.

After checkin' to see if he was fit to travel, I took Barney an' put him in my car. As I began drivin' outta town, he looked at me an' asked the question I knew was comin'.

"So, what are ya gonna do 'bout it, Red?" he pleaded. "That thing is still on the loose an' ya gotta do somethin' to stop it! Yer the law, aintcha? Betty's whole family is gonna blame me unless we get that fucker! I could get the chair if they…"

"Barney, shut up an' let me think, for Chrissake!" I said through the haze o' pain in my head.

I had to go out there an' investigate. Cut an' dried. Barney was no killer. I also knew I had to take Barney with me to do it. I couldn't leave him alone. Everyone in town had heard what he'd said an' news travels fast out here. The Donnens was gonna be callin' for his head 'fore long. They was not a really upstandin' bunch an' they didn't like me for bustin' up a still belongin' to the worst of 'em, Terrence Donnen. Terry had "friends" in high places, too. A local county judge let him go with no fine an' no jail time. Terry was also Betty's uncle. No matter what, this was gonna be messy to clean up an' I decided I needed Barney's help to do it.

I stopped the car just outside o' town an' turned to my passenger an' laid it out for him.

"Barney," I asked with a growl, "Did ya kill the girl outta anger 'cause ya couldn't get yer dick wet?"

He gave me a look like I punched him in his bruised rib. He balled up his fists an' began to pound the seat with them as he spoke.

"No!" he yelled, "Betty an' me was gonna get married soon! Her family wasn't happy 'bout it 'cause I'm just a taxi driver, but we didn't care! We just went out near the blue hole to do some neckin', that's all!"

I'd known Barney since we was kids, an' he'd get squeamish if we shot a squirrel while messin' around in the woods. He was no killer. But I had to prove that – an' to do it, I needed to either find Betty alive wanderin' the woods an' hope this was all mistake or find her body an' see if Barney was lyin'.

I started the car an' put it in gear. Barney asked me what I was plannin' to do. I didn't say anythin' for a few minutes till I got to the old loggin' road out to the blue hole. After I made my turn I told him what I was gonna do.

"Okay, Barney. This is what we're gonna do – an' ya better keep yer head on straight for it." I looked at him hard so he'd get the point. "Yer ass is on the line. We're goin' out there an' yer gonna show me just where she was…" I paused, not believin' the words was comin' outta my mouth, "…eaten or whatever the fuck went on. Let's just hope ya ain't lyin', 'cause that's…"

He started cryin' an' it took me 'back. Was this remorse or fear? My cop's instincts couldn't get a bead on it. He began wailin' like a freshly spanked kid.

"I'm tellin' ya, Red," he blubbered, "it was like I told ya – just a reg'lar night. I picked Betty up an' we saw that one o' them travelin' carnivals had set up in that field next to McKimson's dairy farm. I spent an hour tryin' to win a cupie doll for her an' lost two bucks instead. Betty didn't care, she was just happy to be there with me. We went to see the freaks, an'…"

I stopped Barney there. I didn't need to hear anythin' 'bout his night at the carny. I needed to know how Betty was attacked. Then, again, I thought, maybe they had wild animals – an' maybe that was what was on the loose.

"Barney," I asked, "ya didn't see anythin' like lions or bears at this carnival, did ya?"

Barney looked thoughtful for a second through his tears, an' then shook his head side to side.

"Nope. None that I saw. But there was a dog-faced guy, an' he was…"

"Never mind!" I stopped him. I wasn't in the mood to hear Barney go on an' on again 'bout the carnival. I'd see for myself later. Their kind came through here all the time on their way to the Atlantic City boardwalk. Carnies are worse than gypsies – but if nothin' panned out here, I'd take a sniff.

So, I went back to askin' Barney 'bout his evenin'. "Okay, so what did ya do after ya left the carnival?" Barney licked his lips, swallowed hard an' spoke again. "We had a grand ol' time an' afterward we was feelin' kinda 'frisky', so I drove us out to the blue hole to kinda…well…"

I smiled knowingly, but got him to move the story along.

"Anyways…we was just sittin' there kissin' an' I had my hand up her skirt – but we're engaged an' she'd had a few drinks an' was feelin' good an…"

"She was drinkin'?" I asked him, my suspicion gettin' fanned by the minute – was he or wasn't he comin' clean? "Ya shoulda told me that, Barney," I said, pokin' a finger at him. "Ya shoulda told me right from the start – an' ya might as well tell me right now, 'cause now I'm gettin' mighty suspicious." Barney shifted all uncomfortable in his seat. I didn't have time to dick around. I grabbed his shoulders an' shook him. "Come on, Barney – snap the fuck out of it!" I growled, my anger fueled by the pain in my head. "I'm givin' ya one last chance 'fore I lock ya up or hand ya over to the Donnens. Spill it – all of it!"

"Okay! Okay!" He burbled through his tears. "I was tryin' to keep us outta trouble with ya!"

He knew I had no tolerance for the bootleggers or their customers. "Betty likes the hard stuff an' she got a bottle from her uncle 'fore we went out. I wasn't gonna drink any 'cause the stuff her family makes would give ya the shits an' make ya lose yer sight for day. She was used to it, I guess, 'cause she could drink it like a goldfish could swim in water. Besides, ya know I can't hold my liquor – even if it's the good stuff. Ya remember that Fourth o' July…"

True. Barney was a lousy drunk. The last time was Independence Day two years earlier. He wound up without his pants marchin' down main street singin' "Yank my doodle…it's dandy!" before throwin' up an' passin' out on old Mrs. Markle – who'd been holdin' a sparkler that she dropped on Barney's exposed crotch that set off some real fireworks. After that he wouldn't touch the stuff.

Okay. Now I really had a mystery on my hands. I knew that Barney was tellin' the truth. Ya get lied to a lot in my line o' work an' ya get good at spottin' even the best bullshit stories for what they are. I thought maybe I should call the "staties" in; but this was Barren business, an' Barren business was what I was hired to deal with. Lookin' back now, I probably did the right thing, 'cause what happened next was nothin' anyone could put in a report an' not wind up bein' taken away in a rubber truck.

I drove us to the edge o' the old trail leadin' back to the blue hole. The hole had legends built up 'bout it as the bath o' the Jersey Devil. They say the Devil came here to bathe after it killed an' the clear, blue water could wash even the sins o' the Devil away. Considerin' all the sinnin' that went on from couples skinny dippin' or screwin' there – not to mention the bootleggers who dumped bad batches of hooch into it – it could probably cure more ills than the fountain o' Lourdes.

As we got closer to the old road, Barney was gettin' nervous. The heat was bad enough that day an' he was sweatin' double. Between the humidity an' the stink o' perspiration comin' off Barney, my headache was gettin' worse an' worse. I was determined that no matter what, I was gonna work through the pain an' stay focused.

It was almost seven when I stopped the car an' parked at the mouth o' the trail. The sun would be goin' down soon. I went to the trunk an' took out my flashlight an', more importantly, my Winchester Model 12 pump-action shotgun. The damn thing could hold six shells an' blow a hole big enough to put a badger through a six-point buck. I wasn't takin' chances on just havin' my Colt police revolver with us. After loadin' the rifle I went to get Barney outta the car.

I grabbed the door handle an' told him to get out. He didn't move for a minute an' just stared into the woods. He then looked at the shotgun an' began to yammer 'bout not havin' a way to defend himself. "For shit's sake, Red!" he whined. "What am I supposed to do if that thing comes at me?! Throw fuckin' pine needles? Ya gotta give me a gun! Come on, ya got two an' I got nothin'!"

I didn't know what I was goin' to be meetin' out here – human devil, animal devil or the Devil himself. But all three'd be better than Barney with a loaded gun. "Uh-uh," I told him. "Barney, I wouldn't trust a nervous Nellie like ya with a bean shooter at a boardwalk shootin' gallery. But I'll tell ya what I will do…"

"What's that?" he asked.

"If we see that thing," I said, "I'll make sure ya get a good head start runnin' back to town. Now come on out an' quit pissin' yerself…it's gonna be dark soon!"

He said somethin' under his breath 'bout a syphilitic monkey an' my mother an' got outta the car. I ignored him and headed us off into the woods.

As we got deeper in, it was like they was gettin' denser – almost smotherin'. Drawin' a breath took work, an' walkin' was almost like swimmin' through the air. Barney was havin' a hard time keepin' up. Even that "head start" joke I made wasn't so funny now. I don't think either of us could even get a slow trot goin' from all this wet heat. If there really was a Devil, than he was in the perfect place: 'cause the Barrens in summer truly is Hell.

The other thing 'bout the Barrens is that it's eerily quiet in the deep stuff. I didn't hear birds, squirrels leapin' through the trees or anythin' really. It was so silent that if ya broke a stick with yer foot in the deep stuff ya could hear it for miles. When Barney began to nervously whistle, I was so startled that I almost turned and shot at the noise.

"Barney ya stupid ass! Keep quiet! Ya almost got me…"

That's when I tripped over somethin'. I hit the ground…hard. As I was holdin' my sprained ankle and cursin' the Lord an' all His angels, I started gettin' back on my feet to see what I'd tripped over – which was what was left o' Betty Donnen.

Holy shit – what a sight!

There wasn't so much a body as a pool o', well, Betty. Just a big, ol' mess o' tattered pieces o' dress, splayed out organs, stray bones an' more blood than I'd ever seen. It was all I could do to not puke while lookin' at it – can't say I could say the same for Barney. The stink offa it was not just decomposition an' shit-out intestines, but it also reeked like a barrel o' raw alcohol. An' on top of it all – well, there wasn't no top.

Her head was gone.

Leeds reached over and grabbed the flask. His twenty minutes on the wagon were over. He took a good, long pull, wiped his mouth with the back of his hand and quickly continued, as if afraid that he'd run out o' fuel for his courage as the liquor wore off.

I got my own head on straight an' looked to see where Barney was – I didn't need to see him, all I had to do was follow the sound o' the dry heavin'. I tried walkin' over to the tree he'd braced himself against with one arm while he kept findin' more stuff to empty outta his stomach, but my ankle hurt to beat the band. I figured I had to rest for a second an' let the damned thing stop throbbin' 'fore I needed to run on it – I had a feelin' I'd be needin' to.

"Fuck, fuck, fuck…FUCK!" he was yellin'. He staggered over and dropped to his knees, the smell of his vomit addin' a new angle to the stink. "Look at her! Red…LOOK AT HER!" he moaned, strings o' puke bubbling from his mouth and drooling offa his chin. "It's her all right! I bought that dress for her at Woolworth's last week! Oh God. She's been pulled apart like a Christmas turkey at a prison lunch!" He kept moanin' an' started slappin' around in the mess o' Betty tryin' to find somethin' to hold. I had to get him outta there.

I also knew I had to hide him. People'd find out 'bout this an' he'd be hangin' from a tree or in front o' the courthouse, seein' as how he was the last one to be with her. I decided to try an' walk on my bad ankle. The first step was pure torture, but it started to ease up with each step. I knew, though, if I had to start runnin', then things was gonna get even uglier than they already was. I looked at Barney and knew I needed him for more'n just a witness: I needed him to help us survive whatever the Hell was waitin' out here for us.

"Barney," I said, tryin' to settle him down, "I believe ya an' know that ya could never do it." That seemed to calm him down a bit. "We need to work together," I told him, "an' quickly, 'fore dark completely covers us. Ya try an' get yer shit together while I look around for any tracks or any other clues. Then we'll try an' figure out what to do 'fore we get to town an' I gotta make my report." An', I thought, figure out what the Hell I'm gonna do with ya.

He just nodded numbly an' I winked at him to reassure him. He wasn't havin' none o' that hogwash. He got all puffed up an' demanded that he be given one o' my weapons.

"Yeah? An' while yer putterin' around in the bushes, the Devil will find me an' do what he did to poor Betty." he said, as he stood stiff as a board with a wild look in his eyes. "I ain't movin' or doin' jack snot in a treetop unless ya give me a gun!"

Against my better judgement, an' also 'cause I wouldn't even leave a rabid dog here to fend for itself against an angry grizzly bear after what I saw, I gave in. I figured that the revolver was enough for him. Barney could shoot a pistol, but the shotgun…no way. It was modified an' had a hair trigger. One mistake could kill one of us or both. Although, thinkin' back on it, that might have been more merciful than what happened a little while later.

I threw Barney the Colt an' he gripped it like a drownin' man to a life preserver. While he was busy fondlin' his security blanket – an' hopin' he wouldn't put a hole in me or him – I began to look around in what was left o' daylight. The thick trees would cause dark to fall 'bout half an hour faster than in the open. So with my complainin' ankle I searched the ground near the body for anythin' that would give us a clue as to who or what did this. The first thing I saw was unexpected. It was a hoof print. Actually, it was a series o' dual hoof prints. As a hunter, I knew that any hoofed beast would offer up a set o' two an' two. But all I saw was one set. That made no sense. Add to this that they was spaced further apart than a man's, but still belonged to somethin' that walked on two legs.

I told Barney to keep an eye out for anythin' an' stay put while I moved further away from the scene. Barney did just what I hoped he wouldn't. I heard the hammer on the gun bein' cocked an' made mental note to try an' keep low in case the jittery fuck fired in my direction.

I followed the trail o' weird hoof marks until I found somethin' even stranger. It was a pool o' purple colored slime. An' it wasn't just what it looked like that bugged me: the smell comin' offa it was almost as bad as the stink o' raw booze near the body. As I pinched my nose to bend down closer to look at the stuff I saw what to this day still haunts my sleep.

The hoof tracks turned into a set o' barefoot human footprints. Well, human *lookin'* anyway. They had four toes an' had an elongated heel that made them look like whoever they belonged to was at least a size 16. At least I knew that anyone that big could be easily spotted in a crowd. So even if I couldn't find any other clues or the person themselves, those size 16 brannigans would stand out in a crowd like a turd in a punchbowl. Here was proof that Barney, an average-sized man, was not the killer. I was almost ready to get the Hell outta there when I stopped myself. I had another thought now.

Whoever did this was on horseback. That had to be it! An' ridin' pretty fast, based on the gait o' the tracks. I guess ya'd say I was smug in how I started figurin' it all out in my head. Some bootlegger rode his horse into the deep woods to check on his still – an auto wouldn't make it through. When he got here, he found Barney an' Betty close by an' decided to scare them the Hell outta here. So he rode up near them an' reared his horse up. In the moonlight, it probably looked like somethin' from a pulp horror magazine an' scared the neckin' couple to run in panic. Barney probably went hysterical an' couldn't figure out what was happenin', or went coward, ran to his car, took off an' then later only told me part o' the truth. Poor Betty probably got raped and then left for dead – some wild animal did the rest. With all o' this worked out, I felt triumph – an' sorely pissed off!

I was mad at myself for not beatin' down Barney more to get it all outta him. Stupid rookie mistake – fuckin' headache! I accepted his answers – but they were only half the story. I was goin' to go back to him, to either get it outta his mouth or his hide an' then go lookin' for the bastard bootlegger – they all had their own "smell" an' all I had to do was "follow my nose" to the right brew. An' the right bastard.

I decided to do the second first – leave the little sonofabitch in the dark to stew in his shit-stained drawers a bit. Serves him right, I thought. I started forgin' ahead an', with the bushes an' prickers tearin' at my arms an' clothes, I broke through an' saw the still. Even in the lessenin' light this sucker didn't look like anythin' I'd ever seen. There wasn't the usual couple oo copper or steel kettles connected by spiralin' copper tubin'. This thing looked like…well…it reminded me o' them zeppelins that tied up at Lakehurst in the north o' the state. But this zep looked smaller an' looked like it had a giant fist punched through it. I needed a closer look to figure out what kind o' joy juice factory this was.

As I got closer, I heard somethin' crunch under my shoe. It was gettin' really dark now an' I had to turn on my flashlight. As the electric torch came on I played it around the area o'the sound I saw a skull. An' not just one, but dozens. Most looked to belong to various animals: cows, horses an' assorted small game.

But there was at least five human skulls.

I couldn't tell if anythin' here was recent or had been here for ages. I noticed that quite a few had one thing in common, 'specially the larger animal ones an' the human types: They was all covered in the same purple slime I had seen in that pool 'bout fifty yards away. An' two things was weird. One, everythin' was still wet. Two, the slime was lightly glowin' in the gatherin' gloom. This place would be easier to find in the dark than in the daytime, an' that set up a whole new set o' questions for myself – an' eventually for my interrogation o' Barney. He was out here at dark, so how could he miss…

Just then, a voice rang out in the stillness. Actually, several voices. An' one was way too familiar. I knew it belonged to the one asshole I was hopin' to avoid: the drunken slur o' local bootleg kingpin, Terry Donnen. The Donnens had arrived an' this was goin' to be a whole new shit sandwich with a bite taken outta it. I began to scrabble for the safety o' the thicket I'd come through. I wasn't bein' a coward: I wanted to see if I could catch them red, or, in this case, purple, handed. I had to be sure who caused – or who *didn't* cause – all this mess. After I made sure I was outta sight in the bushes I crouched down, shotgun at the ready, an' settled back on my good heel. The other foot was still throbbin'. So, on my one good appendage, sweatin' an' bein' stung by both prickers an' bloodthirsty Barren mosquitoes, I waited for them to get into the clearin'.

The first one to step into the clearin' was Terry himself. He was a skinny piece o' work: but his thin ass didn't make him any less of a tough bastard. He was built outta steel cord wrapped around a heart an' soul deep an' dark as a cave full o' vampire bats. An' he could fight. I know. I had almost been whipped to death by those lightnin'-fast fists awhile back. Only a foot to his balls had stopped him, an' even that only slowed him down long enough for me to stick my gun up his left nostril an' threaten to blow his head to Timbuktu. Maybe it wasn't honorable, but when the Hell did any street fight for yer life have rules? Anyway, he was no one to fuck with.

I watched as he stood there trainin' a flashlight around the place. Everyplace he didn't light up, the eerie purple glow did. He didn't make a move. He just stood there. An' just when I thought he was goin' to get that light right on me, another three guys came outta the woods behind him. In the dark it was hard to tell who they was. Then Terry spoke up again.

"Jerry, put that bottle o' booze down an' get out one o' them railroad flares ya got. I can't see shit out here!" he growled.

I knew that the Jerry he was speakin' to was his half-witted cousin Jerry Carlyle. Carlyle was a known troublemaker an' I had busted him for petty theft a few weeks earlier. As usual, he got off with a small fine – that an' a larger bribe Terry paid his "pocket judge" for legal disservices rendered. I got pissed thinkin' 'bout that; but I still kept low an' quiet. I wanted to see what that flare was gonna reveal, even though Carlyle balked at usin' the thing.

"Terry, I don't think that's a good idea. What if it sets the woods on fire? It's been awful dry an' hot. It might…"

That's when I heard what had to be the slap of a hand against flesh. I heard Carlyle grunt in pain an' figured that Terry must've driven home his order with a backhand. The extra incentive must've worked, 'cause a few seconds later a red flare lit up the clearin'.

The first thing I did was close my eyes for a bit to adjust to the light after all this dark. When I opened them I got to see the whole area cast in the crimson glow o' the flare. An' all that did was make everythin' look worse than I thought. Not only was there bones everywhere, but they was piled up neat as ya please. I was thinkin' what the Hell went on here – an' Hell was what it was, not any still blowin' up.

The thing I saw had never held a dram o' whiskey. It was long an' silver an' had electrical wires an' other doo-dads the likes o' which I couldn't figure out streamin' from it like one o' them Portuguese Man o' War jellyfish I'd seen washed up on the shore. An' the whole place was littered with bones, scraps o' cloth an' what looked to be a pile o' animal hides near the silver oblong shaped deal. What Terry Donnen said next was the thought that was goin' through my still achin' head.

"Mother o' sweet fuck!" exclaimed Terry, "This is a poacher's camp! I think I know what the Hell's been goin' on around here now!"

At this point, the other two men stepped forward to look. I saw that they was Ray Lonnigan an' "Heinie" Schloss. They was mill hands who had turned to bootleggin' when the mill closed down awhile back. They wasn't bad sorts, just desperate an' worked for the Donnens rather than move away or starve. Pineys would rather die than leave the Barrens.

Ray looked around an' turned to Terry as he said, "Terry, this is more'n poacher's camp! Look at those skulls! Those ain't no animal bones…those are people skulls!"

Terry got a real evil grin on his face an' said, "For the first time in yerr worthless life ya may be on to somethin' an' I know what it is."

Heinie shifted uncomfortably on his feet while his hand went down to the leather sheath on his hip holdin' a long, saw-toothed knife. He was a veteran o' the European trenches and was better'n anyone I'd seen in a knife fight. Terry snarled to him, "Ya get that pig sticker ready for when we catch the sumbitch who did all this! An' if he's the one whose got my sister's kid…I'll help ya carve him from a tree to a toothpick! Carlyle – put out that flare…We're gonna wait for whoever did all this to come back."

He then motioned for his cousin to snuff out the flare.

I tell ya, it was as if Terry had challenged the perpetrator o'this sick scene to show himself, 'cause just as Carlyle stepped forward to do what he was told, somethin' stepped outta the woods opposite all o' them. An' I say "somethin'" not "someone", 'cause what I saw was barely human lookin'. It was 'bout seven feet tall, pale as a ghost, bald as a baby an' with a mouth that seemed to split the lower part of its smooth, hairless face. It was wearin' what looked to be a deer hide tied around its nethers. I tried to get a look at its feet, an' even in that half-light I could see that they was the size o' small canoes. I knew right then an' there this what I'd been trailin' that night. An' the other convincin' thing was what it was holdin' in it's hand.

It was a half-dead chicken.

I was tryin' to figure out my next move, when I heard a shout from my left. Oh fuckshit! Here comes Barney bustin' outta the woods, wavin' my gun around like a crazed cowboy. Goddamn fool! He's gonna muff this whole thing an' probably get killed, too! I was 'bout to get up an' yell that I was there an' arrest the whole kit an' kaboodle when Barney fires the gun at the tall thing holdin' the chicken. He musta missed, 'cause it never even flinched. Instead, it grinned showin' two rows o' needle-lookin' teeth.

An' then it put the head o' the chicken in its mouth an' bit it clean off.

After that, all Hell broke loose. Donnen's men began firin' at the thing. Now, I knew that Terry was good shot, 'cause I'd hunted with him back when we was kids an' he could knock the warts offa toad at thirty yards. Still the thing never flinched an' kept eatin' his early midnight snack. Everythin' got real quiet after the first volley, an' they all stood around gawkin' at the thing with their mouths hangin' open in shock. Heine pulled out that trench knife an' started pacin' 'round the thing in a half crouch, tryin' to find an openin'.

I watched in horror as Heinie finally made his move. He got right up to it, slashed at its belly with his knife an' connected like Babe Ruth swingin' for the bleachers – the thing's guts shoulda come pourin' out. But the gash seemed to close on itself as he was makin' it. Heinie froze. As a matter o' fact, no one moved: me included. I didn't know what the Hell to do either! This was the nuttiest thing ever – an' just when I thought it couldn't get any fuckin' weirder...

It did.

The thing's mouth opened in a huge, awful grin an' a long, snakelike tongue came out an' licked around its lips – if that's what ya wanna call them. Just as the flare was dyin' out I saw what sent me screamin' to the bottom of a bottle, where I've stayed to this day. The thing began to shake an' its skin began to look like it was bubblin' as if it was boilin' from within. Then, an' I swear to good Christ above, it began to *change*.

It got taller. An' the baby like face got longer an' began to look like a starved horse's does. It was long an' the skin was stretched tight. The ears – what might or mightn't have been – went right on top of its head an' looked like two curvy horns. Then the legs began to get longer an' crooked like a dog's hind legs. The big-ass feet turned into dishpan-sized hooves, too. But that wasn't the worst of it: its back seemed to spread out like ya see a bat when it takes flight.

An' just like a bat, two huge wings sprung from it!

'fore anyone could react, it loomed up over Heinie an' faster than nothin' I'd seen 'fore or since, that ugly ass horse head's lower jaw opened wider'n a whore's thighs an' slammed down over the German's head clear to his shoulders. I heard Heinie's muffled scream, a sickenin' crack an' then he fell to the ground. Well, not all of him – his head was still in the thing's mouth an' it was suckin' on it like a piece o' rock candy.

No one budged. No one said a damn thing. We all just stood where we was, listenin' to that ungodly suckin' – until Barney yelled out, "That's it! That's the thing that killed Betty! Get it! For God's sake, shoot it…shoot it again! IT'S THE GODDAMN DEVIL!!!"

The thing that had killed Betty an' Heinie sniffed the air, roared like a lion an' began to move toward Terry an' his crew. They raised their rifles an' fired. Just then the flare went out.

All I could see was the flash o' gun barrels an' hear the screams o' that thing mixed in with human cries. I heard bullets whippin' past me like bees headin' for the hive. There was a slurpin' sound an' more screams that could have waked all the dead on this shore an' the one across the fuckin' sea. There was more flashes o' gunfire. I steeled myself – I had to do somethin', even if it killed me. It was my job an' I damn well was gonna do it!

I pumped a round into the shotgun an' went to turn on my flashlight. Even if I hit one o' the guys out there, it couldn't be worse than what I knew was happenin' to them. Maybe, I thought for a flash of a second, that it would be mercy that was needed for them. It would be better to die from a bullet than what that sick fuck was doin' to them! Just as I was gonna try an' shine the light into the clearin' an' see if some 12-gauge shells could do what all the other ammo hadn't, I heard a sound like a dull flute. 'fore I could figure out where this new noise was comin' from, somethin' hit me in the back o' the head an' I went out like a light in a thunderstorm.

Dr. Sarcophagus was still quietly sitting across from Leeds, who was now sobbing into his hands. Reflexively, he reached again for the flask and drank…and drank. His moment of reform had come and gone with the completion of his story. Now, all he wanted to do was drown the memory deep beneath the waves of liquorish nepenthe.

Even the bottomless finds a bottom, and Leeds eventually had to stop to breathe. "Damn!" he said, gasping for air and staring at the flask. "Does that thing ever run outta booze?" Dr. Sarcophagus smiled and replied, "Its magic is not in what it holds, but in what it fills. Whatever is most empty in the one who drinks is that which is filled until the drinker is, shall we say, complete again."

Leeds gave a wan smile through his tears. "Well, that's some pretty powerful sorcery, Doc. I don't feel drunker an' I actually don't feel like havin' anymore. Actually, I just feel kinda tired an' a bit sad. But that's all. For the first time in years I don't want to drink till I'm numb. Ya think the magic fixed me up? Could it be, Doc?" Before the doctor could answer, Leeds looked pleadingly into his companion's calm visage and begged, as he held his head in his hands, "Please tell me what the Hell is goin' on! Please tell me I ain't goin' nuts!"

Shaking and holding his bowed head, weeping, his voice trailed off into "Please…please…please…" getting softer, wetter, childlike.

Dr. Sarcophagus did something unexpected. He slid his chair, squeaking on the floorboards, over near Leeds' and put an arm around his shoulder. Leeds nestled his head onto the man's chest and continued to silently sob. A slow cacophony of jeers began to rise from the crowd – but Leeds never saw the look that the doctor fanned out at the collected, one that none who were there that night would remember without reaching for liquid comfort.

Returning to Leeds he said, "Red, life has done you great injustices. You've suffered for some foolish mistakes that were no fault of your own. I'm here to, as Puck said, make amends. But before all of that, you need to tell me."

"Tell ya?" Leeds said confused, lifting his head off of Dr. Sarcophagus. "Tell ya what, exactly?"

The doctor corked the flask, put it away in his coat pocket and inquired as to what had happened after that horrible night. Leeds told him that the next day he woke up in his car with Barney sitting on the seat next to him. Both of his weapons were there, as well the Colt pistol – and neither looked as if they had been fired! The pistol had all of its bullets and the shotgun didn't show any signs of discharge or damage. Unfortunately, the same couldn't be said of Barney – he was catatonic.

He left Barney to go back to the clearing. What he saw terrified him more than what had happened the night before. Or had it?

The long silver cylinder, the bones – everything – even all of the footprints and tracks were gone. He called out to see if any of the Donnen crew was around, but all he heard was the usual profound silence that was the Barren's trademark. Nothing but the wind whispering through the trees.

Leeds went back to the car. Barney was still unmoving and unblinking. Knowing what shock looked like, Leeds grabbed an old blanket from the back of his car, wrapped it around his companion and drove back into town – where his worst fears were realized. Someone, probably Donnen's wife, had called the state police. Leeds was questioned for hours. He told them everything; but when they saw the knot on the back of his head, they chalked his wild tale up to concussion-induced hallucinations. Barney was of no help, alternating between silence, repeating Betty's name and then breaking into uncontrollable shrieking.

Barney. He spent the few, short remaining months of his life in a sanitarium up near Trenton. One day, an attendant found him bled out – he had torn out the veins in his wrists with his teeth. They never found Terry Donnen and his men – and it was a poorly kept secret that no one looked very hard. Everyone got paid to keep their mouths shut. Things were not good in the country and Atlantic City was still a popular place for the wealthy to spend their money. The last thing anyone needed was wild tales of the Jersey Devil on a rampage through the southern part of the state to chase away that income.

Leeds? He became the unspoken fall guy. They forced him into retirement, gave him his pension and essentially let it be known that a crime had gone unsolved and unpunished because of his negligence. What crime? No one knew – or was supposed to. That was all fine and well with Leeds. He sank to the bottom of a bottle in the hopes that someday he could drink himself into blissful unknowing. Try as he might, it never happened.

Dr. Sarcophagus sat thoughtfully for a moment and then reached into his pocket. When he brought it out again it held a small leather bag tied at the top. He opened Leeds' hand, placed the bag in it and gently closed the man's fingers around it.

"What's this for?" Leeds asked. Dr. Sarcophagus gave a warm smile, pulled his wire-rimmed glasses down his aquiline nose and said smoothly, "As a fellow aficionado of the Great Bard, consider it a gift from 'one poor player' to another – the 'amends' to which I earlier alluded." Leeds opened his mouth to speak, but Sarcophagus cut him off. "Please. Do not ask – for I cannot fully explain. But let this be a meager recompense for wrongs done against you by society. And, sadly, by me."

Leeds' eyes grew wide; his mouth fell slackly open. "What? Ya sayin' ya had somethin' to do with all this shit?" he said stunned. "That can't be!" he said, confused and agitated, "I ain't never laid eyes on ya 'fore tonight. I can't take this, Doc. I may be a drunk an' all but I ain't no grifter!" He began pushing the bag back across the table and was stopped by the doctor's cane suddenly resting between them.

Dr. Sarcophagus shook his head to the negative and said, "Mr. Leeds, think of this as your new retirement – one which you truly deserve. It contains some very ancient gold, which, if you bring it to a man I know on Canal Street in New York, he will pay you enough in modern U.S. currency for you to retire in style." When Leeds attempted to renew his argument, Sarcophagus stood up and placed his hand on the man's shoulder.

"'If we shadows have offended, think but this, and all is mended,'" he said in a whisper.

The words echoed in Leeds' head like the patter of water dripping on wet stone in a cave, lulling him into a hypnotic peace. The shatter of a glass and a vulgar oath brought him back to reality. The crowd was its raucous, drunken self – and Leeds was alone. He ran a hand through his shock of red hair and wheeled around in his chair – his erstwhile companion was gone.

He was almost ready to ask himself if Dr. Sarcophagus had ever even existed, or if he was some drunken vision – until he saw the pouch on the table. His hands shaking, he picked up the pouch, which had considerable heft for something so small, and undid the drawstring. Wordlessly, he re-sealed it, stood up and announced that he had to catch a bus to New York. He gave a brief smirk at the absence of reaction and walked out of Club Elite's doors, never to return to it or the Barrens.

As for Dr. Sarcophagus, he was never seen in the Barrens again.

After leaving the club, Dr. Sarcophagus returned through the tree-filled night to the carnival. No sooner had he passed within its tent-lined confines, than he was greeted by one of his assistants, a dwarf named Thomas, who breathlessly wheezed, "Doc! Thank the gods you're back! You know what 'he' gets like when you're not around – especially where we are!"

Dr. Sarcophagus gave his frantic friend a benign smile and said soothingly, "Thomas, please. Calm down. All is well...now."

Thomas was one of the few who could speak his mind to the doctor. He threw his hands up in the air and said sarcastically, "Well *ain't* that juuuust *ducky*?! All hail you!" Dr. Sarcophagus stood with an amused grin while his assistant stormed around ranting, "While you've been out wandering around it's been a chore to keep 'you know who'–"

"The 'geek'," corrected Dr. Sarcophagus.

"...the 'geek'," continued Thomas with a sneer, "in line – as usual. He knows he's near his home and has been trying to get out of here." Before the doctor could reply, Thomas went on without an inhalation.

"*Anddddd*...he and Bartleby – well, Bartleby – have been lookin' for a re-match!" Thomas said sternly, "It's almost the full moon and I caught him trying to toss a bottle of liquor into the geek's tent! If that thing changes and Bartleby changes then we might as well shut down forever – the last time those two tangled this whole place was almost turned into goulash!"

Thomas stood staring, exhausted by his dramatic soliloquy. Sarcophagus grew quiet for a moment. He thought back to that evening with a frown – but then his entrepreneurial mind thought that the gate from a match between a werewolf and the infamous Jersey Devil would ensure his retirement and the safety of his family in perpetuity. He quickly chided this fantasy, which was replaced by the sober realization that he had to get the carnival away from this place forever.

But there was a bit of unfinished business.

He turned to his assistant and said, " Dear Thomas. As usual, you are reason's voice." The little man looked up at his boss and sardonically replied, "Yeah, well, someone has to run this show like a business, not his personal museum manned by poor relatives."

"Too true, too true," chuckled Dr. Sarcophagus. "Here's what we need to do. Tell Bartleby that if he doesn't stop, I'll make him count all of the silver coins we get for the next ten shows. Then, get the geek ready for travel."

Thomas was perplexed. "Where?"

"Home," replied Dr. Sarcophagus, placing a hand on Thomas' shoulder. "His real home. Tell me: you did…*acquire* that surveyor's map of the cavern and sinkhole system of the area, yes?"

Thomas nodded. He now knew what the doctor had planned. Thomas had been in on the whole thing seven years earlier when they found the geek wandering around the carnival. The thing had been attracted by the sound of Dr. Sarcophagus playing on his ocarina, which he was wont to do to relax after a performance. Only the doctor and Thomas had seen it – and Bartleby.

The creature ambled up to Dr. Sarcophagus like a mortal entranced by Orpheus himself. It stood there with what amounted for a smile, listening – until Bartleby wandered past with an open bottle of whiskey (which he was forbidden from drinking during a full lunar phase – not that he ever listened). One sniff of the aroma was enough to initiate its transformation from childish being to devilish, horrific beast. The fight that ensued as the now devil and the enraged werewolf wrestled over the bottle of liquor would have torn them and the carnival to pieces, had not the creature been re-calmed by the sound of the ocarina and Bartleby with Thomas' shouted promise of a case of moonshine.

The thing reverted back into its more sedate form and ran off into the Barrens. Dr. Sarcophagus and Thomas chased after it, which is how they came to be the unwitting witnesses of the Donnen incident. Rather than seeing the creature as a threat, the doctor felt it to be simply another unfortunate victim of fate and wanted to prevent it from harming itself or others. Unfortunately, the strong smell of alcohol on the Donnens reawakened the "devil" that ultimately killed them all.

Dr. Sarcophagus knocked Leeds unconscious with his cane and calmed the creature with his music. Thomas cleaned the entire area – his prodigious strength helped to make the job easier than expected. Like so many at the carnival, Thomas was not what he seemed to be.

During the expunging of the evidence, they determined the origin of the creature: beneath the ruined cylinder – which turned out to be a kind of steam-powered, turbine-driven drill – was a gaping hole in the earth. Some mechanical genius with a hare-brained scheme to dig for mineral deposits must have uncovered a cave system within which this creature had existed. As they learned, the "geek," as they called it, could eat and digest almost any substance, so it must have subsisted on plants, animals – even rocks – within its dark home.

The geek could not process alcohol, though, regardless of it source or concentration. Sarcophagus put it on display as a miracle of evolution, able to eat anything – hence the term "geek." Anything, that is, but comestibles that contained alcohol. For the past seven years, it had made him considerable money while being well taken care of and protected. Was it alone? Dr. Sarcophagus and Thomas never ventured to guess. From whence had it come? Neither could say. But it had sprung from the earth and to the earth it needed to be returned. The doctor had always intended to do so after seeing the destruction that evening. He knew it had never been meant to walk in the light of the sun or the moon, and that the time would come when he would have to set things right.

And that time was now.

Dr. Sarcophagus came out of his reverie and heaved a great sigh. "Thomas," he said, "Please bring that map and meet me behind my wagon, where I will be waiting with a family member who needs to return, at last, to his true home – and, perhaps, his true family." Thomas nodded and ran to his tent.

As he watched him round a corner and disappear from sight, Dr. Sarcophagus took out his ocarina, wet his lips and began to play, filling the Barren night with a tune by his old friend, Felix.

𝕋𝔼ℕ𝕋 𝟼

SAVING GRACE
Dee Langford

Through the closed curtains, I hear them entering the small, dark tent. I eavesdrop on their conversations: most I have heard in one form or another over the years. My courage grows as I listen to men who chose or were chosen to be at my show and to hear my story. It is not easy, this thing I do. I do it because I need to – because they need me to.

"Shit. I just told her that I was gonna see what I was gonna see and if she didn't like it she'd like it a Hell of a lot less when I got back home. Then that weird guy who runs this place, Dr. Sarcophagus, stops me. Says I seem like the kind of man who would enjoy this show. Damn right! He sure knows…"

"Mine wanted to come to the fair, but whined she didn't have anything to wear. She sure shut up when I told her she had a whole closet full of clothes, but was too damn fat to wear them."

"…you got a free ticket, too?" asks another voice from behind the closed curtains. This one sounds like a young man, a boy even.

"Whatcha doin' in here? You're just a kid. A little young for this show, ain't ya?"

"I'm old enough to do your wife better than an old geezer like you!" The teenager shoots back to laughter. "Besides, just like that other guy, that strange Dr. Sarcophagus gave me a ticket. It's weird. I thought I was gonna be kicked out when this big bouncer guy caught me having some fun. Did you see that cat running around with the firecracker tied to its tail?"

I prepare to begin the show. I remind myself that I am a different person now: stronger, better. And I tell myself that not all men are like these men; that the men sitting in the audience were gathered tonight for a purpose. Some were chosen by Dr. Sarcophagus, while others were unknowingly drawn to my tent. They are all driven by the same hidden desires, a hunger that makes it their destiny to be here.

With a nod to Alfie standing in a corner behind me, the lights are dimmed once, twice, three times: the signal that the show is about to start. I hear the rustle as people settle into their seats. The lights go out altogether and a moment later the curtains are slowly pulled open.

I am seated on a chair in the middle of the stage. I like the vision of me sitting on a damask chair in front of a small makeup table like you might find in a woman's bedroom. But right now, all the crowd can see is my face.

"Good evening and welcome to my show. I am Grace," I wait for five beats and continue, "the Tattooed Lady." And then suddenly the lights come up and there are gasps as I stand and reveal myself to them.

"I never understand why people are so surprised when they first see me. You paid to see a tattooed lady and I am certainly that – tattooed from head to toe – although some might dispute my using the word 'lady' to describe me." I laugh and the men slyly chuckle along with me. "As for the tattoos, in case you are wondering," I pause as I slowly pirouette in front of them, "yes, I have tattoos on my front and on my back."

Tonight I am wearing my sheer, pale blue peignoir with nothing underneath save my tattoos and a pair of panties and pasties – for even we won't go any farther. As I turn in front of them, they can see glimpses of my colorful tattoos flashing beneath my robe before I daintily sit back down.

On the surface, it seems almost normal: a beautiful, barely dressed woman seated on an elegant chair. My long, black hair loosely flows behind my robe as if I had just unpinned it for the night in the privacy of my bedroom. I cross my legs exposing one long, well-shaped leg covered in tattoos from my ankle to as far as they can see. And it hits the crowd that I am what they cruelly call a "freak", a spectacle – and it simultaneously repulses and intrigues them. The effect is much stronger than if I had greeted them in a sleazy outfit sitting on a plain stool as I have seen other tattooed ladies do. Dr. Sarcophagus has taught me well, how to emphasize my differences by presenting myself in an almost normal situation.

Once again, they realize that I am not just any woman. I still feel their desire wafting up at me in the scent of the musk of lust, with a subtle hint of violence. They are angry that I have caused them to desire me. They also acknowledge the fact that I am up here alone; one, vulnerable woman surrounded by a sea of masculinity. Enough already: it is time now to bring them into my life.

"Gentlemen and ladies," I start. I always begin with that introduction, even though there are never any females in the audience. "Perhaps you wonder how it is that I became what you see before you? Certainly, as a little girl, or even young lady, I didn't announce that I wanted to grow up to be a tattooed lady." I make this joke to help relax the crowd a bit, my girlish giggle eliciting a similar response from the men.

I let the silence return before proceeding. "What you see is my life. Some people express their experiences on paper or canvas – but I have the ability of neither a Twain nor a Gauguin." I drink in the blank looks on the faces – my confidence is bolstered by their ignorance. "No, instead I wanted the world to see what it had made me, for I am a product of all of my experiences." I wave my arm up and down my body with a slow flourish and, with a sly smile, add, "As you can tell, I am very experienced." Ah, "experienced" – the men in the room all start to whistle and hoot at me, slapping each other on the back and making not-so-silent oaths of what they would do to me to add to my experience. But, because they are men, they do not understand – or choose to not understand – the many definitions of the word.

I bite down hard on my disdain. Suddenly, the room goes dark except for a small spotlight on my outstretched right hand. "We begin my story in tattoos with something as simple as a finger – or many fingers." Everything is plunged back into pitch black, except for a small spotlight on my outstretched right hand. "Do you see? There is a dark red tattoo on these fingers; thick red lines, marring my pale skin, circling 'round and 'round each. Cruel marks emphasizing the ugly black, blue and green shades of a nasty bruise permanently etched onto my hand.

"These tattoos represent the injuries I received when I tried to protect myself the first time I faced evil. I was young and beautiful – and I was a whore." Snickers and catcalls erupt from the audience. Suddenly, I have become more, how shall I put it, "possible". I ignore them. "Yes, a whore. At the time, I told myself that this oldest occupation was only a temporary thing, although little did I know that this is what all young whores tell themselves. But let me tell you about Harvey. Oh yes, I remember your names, every one of you.

"Harvey was rough – and my first. He was not into subtleties or even the pretense that this was a romantic encounter. It was raw. I was still so very young and innocent, and Harvey made me feel like the whore that I was. He didn't even remove his shirt, much less his shoes or socks. Standing in front of me, he unzipped his pants and pushed them down to his ankles. He grabbed me by my hair forcing me to kneel in front of him" – growls and woofs from the pack of an audience before me – "as he sat heavily on the side of the bed. Oral sex? This was a new request and seemed repugnant to me. He smelled rank from lack of bathing and the thought of what he wanted disgusted me. Placing my hand on his chest I tried to push to get up and away from him. Harvey grabbed my hand and with little thought and no remorse snapped the bones in my middle three fingers."

"I screamed in pain while he gripped my broken fingers even tighter in his fist. He used his other hand to push my head down – and that is when I noticed that this violence had made him excited. This was my first encounter with a man who was aroused in this manner. It was not to be my last. And so that night, defeated and in pain, I did what Harvey demanded. Gagging and choking, it seemed to take forever as I fumbled in my disgust and ineptitude. Of course, it finally ended; but the memory of that encounter is still raw. And to make sure I never forget it, I have these tattoos to remind me." I barely finish when the spotlight suddenly goes out then reappears on my face.

The men are equally aroused. They thrive on sex and violence.

"Fortunately, though, I always had the good looks you see now," I say, as I slowly turn around, letting my hands wander along my skin under my peignoir. "One of my 'customers' was more than talk when he said that he would 'take me away from all of this': he was, in fact, the president of Willows Cosmetics.

"You see this tattoo – here? The one threading its way up my spine? It is a willow tree. I have its roots all the way down to the crease between my buttocks to remind me of how being the Willows Girl meant having to sell my ass – only legitimately." The men all crane their heads to look; but I tease them and turn around before they can only catch a quick glimpse. Good. So begins the lesson in frustration.

"Johnson Graham promised me the world – and, at first, it seemed like it was true. But that world grew darker when he hired my brother, Jack, to help organize my final trip as Willows Girl to Japan.

"Jack was my older brother, who had snaked his way into many of the right parties and cozied up to many of the right people. Johnson Graham was impressed with precisely that – his ability to put the shine on people – and, since he was my brother, Graham figured he would keep it 'all in the family' and make Jack my manager."

I gesture for more light and point to what look like branches on the tree. Instead, once they are illuminated, it is obvious what they are: crosshatched scars covered with tattoos. "Yes, this is how Jack 'managed' me: with a belt."

"Yeah," I hear a man in the front row guffaw to his neighbor, loud enough for everyone to hear, "that's what I said to my wife when she wised off at me the second day we were married and I gave her a metal buckle across her mouth – 'You're under new management, sweetheart!'" All of the other men burst out into uproarious laughter. I sit down and turn to gaze into my dressing mirror as if I were alone in my bedroom putting on my makeup. The laughter dies down and one man yells out, "Hey, sister! More skin and less bullshit!" I turn to him and say with a nonchalant wave of my hand, "In that case, maybe you should leave – then the others will have more of the first and less of the latter."

The man stands up, fuming – ah, the quick-tempered abuser. I know him well. Alfie steps forward. There are few who will do more than stand up when confronted by nearly 350 lbs. of muscle. He sits back down to giggles and chortles from his fellows.

And my narrative begins.

So, yes. As I was saying. I was the Willow Girl for quite some time, my face adorning all of their promotions. Eventually, though, models, like whores, become too old and are replaced by younger versions. And so, at 27, I was becoming too old to be the Willows Girl and, truth be known, I was happy to relinquish that title to a younger woman. But before that could happen, I had one last, major event: Willows entry into the Japanese market. To finalize and celebrate the deal, a number of us would be traveling to Japan. The group included Johnson Graham; Abigail Willows, owner of Willows Cosmetics; and Robert Owens, the head of Owens Advertising, which managed all marketing and branding for the account.

Of course I had to go, as they wanted the Willows Girl to be a part of all of the events and I was still that girl. I had been looking forward to this trip and hoped that I would have some free time to sightsee. A few weeks before we left, I mentioned my interest to Owens. I was shocked by his outburst.

"By no means will you be allowed to wander around by yourself!" he huffed. "Japan is a civilized country where no proper woman, especially an unmarried one, goes out alone. Nor is it acceptable for a lone woman to talk to a strange man or, for that matter, woman. You must be chaperoned at all times, which is why I have invited your brother to come with us. So from the moment we step on Japanese soil until we return to the boat, you are Jack's responsibility. Do what he says and try not to create any scandals while we are there."

As you can imagine, I was stunned. I couldn't imagine a worse situation. My hopes and plans for this trip died. Then I thought, no, I am going to enjoy this trip and I will not let them take this away from me. I knew Jack wouldn't be able to resist seeing me one last time before we left and for once I was going to fight back. Maybe this time I'll teach him a lesson and then he'll leave me alone here *and* in Japan! I thought about buying a gun; but, no, I couldn't do that. I didn't want to kill him, just make him stop abusing me. 'So I took a knife from my kitchen and put it under my pillow. Could I even use this on him? I didn't have long to wait to find out – a few nights before our departure, he visited my apartment. I could smell the liquor on him.

"Hi sis, all ready for the big trip? I sure am. You want to know why? What, no guesses? Then let me tell you…" He was beaming from ear to ear. I just walked away from him and into the bedroom. He stormed after me screaming, "Don't you turn your back on me, you little bitch! Or should I say 'whore?' Isn't that how you got this sweet, little deal with Graham?"

I could feel the anger burning in me. Oh yes, I will be able to use the knife. I would not let him hurt or control me anymore. Jack had already begun removing his belt and was reaching for my arm to pull me closer – he didn't see me reach under the pillow and tightly grasp the handle of the knife.

"On this trip you are mine!" he yelled. "Every move you make has to first be approved by me. You won't even be able to take a shit without asking for my permission. Do you understand me? Owens told me all about it. Said Japanese women stay home, never leaving unless they are with their husband or father or…brother. We wouldn't want you to embarrass us, now would we? Just to be sure you've learned your lesson, I think you need a reminder."

It was then that he grabbed me – and I stabbed him.

With a shriek, I brought the knife down on his thigh, savoring the sickening feeling of metal penetrating flesh. I yanked it out with a thick popping noise and then buried it in his arm. He didn't have time to scream until the second stab.

"You bitch!" Jack howled, as he tried to remove the knife sticking out from his arm.

I hadn't thought past stabbing him – now what? Where do I go?" I ran to the living room.

"Nowhere" was the answer, for Jack had pulled the knife out and, with it still dripping his blood, had followed me out. I was a dead woman. I was frozen and easy for him to grab. He hurled me headlong across the room into a coffee table. Jack stood above me and cocked his foot to kick me.

Instead of taking the hit, I was able to reach out, grab his foot and yank it out from underneath him. He fell down next to me, groaning in pain when his wounded arm hit the table, splattering it with a mist of blood. I struggled to stand up, but Jack reached up and grabbed me by my hair, pulling me down again. But he was now no longer holding the knife – he had dropped it when he fell. The advantage was mine as I snatched it and pointed it right under his nose.

"I will slice your nose off if you move," I hissed. "This has got to stop – and it's going to stop with either you or me dead. At this point, I don't care if it's me, because then your gravy train goes dry.

"I backed away, still holding the knife in his direction, and started inching towards the phone. That's when he said something unexpected.

"You hurt me!' he whined drunkenly. "Whatcha do that for? I never hurt you. Just a few whippin's! Hell, Pa whipped me nearly every day of my life till I got out of there and it ain't nothing. Geez, sis, you didn't have to go use a knife."

"What a pussy!" yells someone from the crowd. "If I were him, I would really show you who's the boss, not sit there whining!" More voices rise up in agreement as they call my brother various names. I interrupt them to get back to my story.

Jack. I didn't want to do it – but you made me! I'm a grown woman – this ends now."

More frightening than if he had attacked me, he simply left without saying another word. I knew this wasn't the end of it – the question that gnawed at me was when would he strike back?"

The next ten days blocked those thoughts: ten whirlwind days of preparation, ending when we finally boarded a liner for Europe, our first stop on our trip. Abigail and I were the only women on the ship, and I had a small suite next to hers, while Jack was on another floor.

The first day on board we met for breakfast in Abigail's suite. I hadn't seen much of Jack and so I was unprepared for the ugly red scar on his arm where I had knifed him nearly two weeks prior. Apparently, no one else had seen Jack in short sleeves and they asked him about the scar. I waited anxiously to hear what he would say.

"Some asshole pulled a knife on me at a bar a few weeks ago. Fast little bugger; but I managed to swerve, so he just caught my arm. The bastard got away that night. Just as I was going to go after him some of his friends grabbed me. It took three of them to hold me back while the lying son of a bitch took off. I didn't worry though. I know where he lives so I figured I would pay him a visit when we get back. No hurry about it and the longer the wait, the less prepared he will be and the greater the surprise. Then I will teach him a lesson he won't ever forget cuz nobody pulls a knife on me and gets away with it!"

Jack spoke those last words with his eyes locked on mine. A chill swept over me in spite of the warm, summer's morning. Why had I thought that I might have stopped my brother? Why couldn't I leave well enough alone? As Jack had said, a few whippings weren't that awful, whereas I now feared that he just might kill me. Every night his threats stalked my thoughts and invaded into my dreams. I grew thinner and jumpier, afraid of everything and not trusting anyone.

Meanwhile, even with his boss on board, Graham still managed to break away and party with my brother. Just when I could have most used a friend, Abigail became colder and colder to me. It didn't matter how much I disapproved of Jack or how little control I had over his actions – she still basically blamed me for him being my brother. And being on the trip.

The next two weeks were a blur to me. Endless train and boat rides interspersed with promotional events. It went on and on and on. Finally, after the hassle of finding all of the luggage, boarding a train and then taking cars, we arrived at our destination – the new Imperial Hotel designed by Frank Lloyd Wright. I was brought to a lovely room on the second floor, with a large glass window overlooking the reflecting pond. As I suspected, my room was next to my brother's; but, to my relief, the adjoining door had a lock that I quickly fastened.

We were given the next twenty hours to rest. The following morning, we were picked up to take a tour of their flagship department store. Matsumoto

Goro, the owner of the department store, and a half a dozen of his top executives were waiting for us. The store was beautiful, catering to the growing upper class in Tokyo, and I could see why it was picked to sell Willows Cosmetics.

After our tour, we were taken to the executive dining room for lunch. I had a feeling that few women had ever been inside this room, based on the looks we were getting from some of the executives. I happened to sit next to Goro. He was a stern and imposing man in his mid sixties. My years as an escort (or more) for men just like him were excellent preparation. I had a lovely time chatting with him, and it seemed as if he enjoyed himself, too.

Meanwhile, Jack and Graham dispensed with the Japanese delicacies in lieu of a "liquid lunch" – and it was beginning to show. The waiters even tried to exchange the sake for hot tea, but the two men rudely waved the solicitous staff away demanding more of the harder stuff. Abigail and Owens kept glaring at me, as if I had any control over my brother. I did try to gently suggest they try the tea, but Jack turned on me.

"That's my dear sis: always trying to henpeck me. God! Who needs a wife when she's around? See, Gracie? The Japs have it figured out: their women stay home and obey what the men say!"

I was mortified. I was embarassed for myself and for Goro. If I could have, I would have crawled under the table. Abigail looked like she wanted to do to him what I did before we left for Japan.

After lunch, the executives of both companies met, while I wandered through the department store buying a few things for myself and friends back home. We were given a tour of the city, and I was glad to get back to my room at the Imperial to take a bath and relax. Fortunately, dinner was a "men-only" affair, of which I was very glad. So, I luxuriated in the hot water for what felt like a glorious eternity before lounging on the bed. That peace was shattered when I heard Jack rattle the adjoining door.

"You in there Gracie? How'd ya like lunch? Too bad you're gonna miss out on the dinner. But don't worry sis, I'll come back and tell ya all about it." I said nothing. Then, there was a questioning tapping on the door, and I could tell that Jack had his mouth pressed right up to it as he half-whispered, "Gracie…oh, Gracie! Do you think a lock is going to stop me? Should I come over and teach you a lesson tonight? Do you think I'm crazy enough to touch you here and now? Fuck no. But you'll still wonder every night if this is the night? And you're gonna check your door and jump at every little noise thinking is that me coming to get ya? And then once we're back home…Damn, this is gonna be fun. I'm gonna whup your ass and make you regret you ever pulled that knife on me. For ya know what they say, right? 'Payback's a bitch', little sister – payback's a BITCH with claws and teeth!"

Jack gave the door a good, solid kick before he left. It was a long time before I finally drifted off to sleep.

"I was awakened by men's voices. I had been in a deep slumber and was a bit groggy, yet I still easily identified the voices as Jack's and Graham's. I assumed that they had returned from their evening, for it seemed quite late. As usual, they were drunk enough that their voices carried into my room. It was so dark as I sat up in bed to listen, but it seemed like...

Then I felt hands on my shoulders pushing me back down onto the bed. Oh my God! They were here, in my room! No, no, no, it wasn't possible!

"'Didn't think I could get in here, did you sis?" Jack hissed in the dark. "Now, see, that's where you underestimate me – something you do far too often. For here we are, checking in on you. Right, Graham?"

"Oh yeah, Jack, I think it's time I checked on all of her. Now turn on the light and let's see what we have here,'" slurred Graham.

Shading my eyes from the sudden brightness of the light, I saw Graham hovering next to my bed while my brother stood beside the yawning, adjoining door.

"Remember what I said, dear sister of mine?" Jack sneered. "I think it just might be payback time – right here and now!" Never in my life had I felt such abject disgust and horror as I did that first moment when, through clearer vision, I saw my brother standing there without his pants or underwear, stroking a solid erection. "Oh, this? This is a little somethin' special for you, sis – but it'll have to wait, cuz I told Graham he could go first…"

Graham was on top of me and, as I opened my mouth to scream, it was filled with his tongue. At the same time, I was barely aware of Jack warning me that it would go much worse for me if I screamed. It was then that I saw the knife in Jack's hand. Graham pulled his mouth off of mine and smiled evilly. "Come on, baby. It'll be just like old times – only better!"

"That's right," Jack said, "Once a whore always a whore!"

"Enough already!" shouted Graham, fumbling with his pants. "'I came here to fuck, not to talk!

Jack came over and sliced off my nightgown. Graham grabbed the knife from Jack's hand and said, "Oh, look! Someone wants to play!" as he began to trace a circle around a hardening nipple.

Oh God oh god oh god. If he slipped, the knife could cut it off. It didn't help that the cold and fear had caused my nipples to tighten up into small, hard buds. I begged him to stop. He simply laughed and dug the edge around the areola, drawing blood and making me scream.

"Don't like that either, whore? Well, now let's see how you're gonna like this…" Graham whispered in my ear.

I felt the knife move slowly down my body. I was afraid to move, to even breath. I groaned as the knife barely pierced my skin, drawing a thin slice etched with a tracing of blood. The pain was nothing compared to the horror that came next, when I felt the tip of the knife first circle then gentle sit barely inside my vagina. I wanted to scoot up and away, but before I could move he told me if I stayed still I wouldn't get hurt – or at least not as badly hurt as I would if I moved.

"Hey, Jack!'" snickered Graham, "I think she likes it! Get your ass over here and get a piece of this!"

Rape. Every woman fears that word. The horror of losing control and being at the mercy of a dangerous man. And that night Graham brutally raped me. He was so large and my vagina was so dry – the agony was indescribable as he tried to force himself inside me, tearing me.

"You needed you a real man, baby!" shouted someone from the audience.

"I'd make you so wet you'd be coming all over yourself!" yelled another.

I continued to talk, ignoring the audience, knowing they would quiet down to hear me.

Graham grunted at my unyielding flesh and demanded that I suck him. He mounted my face – I couldn't resist if I wanted to – and thrust himself into my mouth. I choked and gagged for breath, fighting off the urge to vomit as he clogged my airway.

"Ooh. That's it. All nice and wet," Graham moaned as he pulled out of my mouth and mounted me again. His penis was even larger, but now with my saliva on it he was able to slide it in me. But it wasn't sliding – it was pummeling, over and over. Oh God, it hurt so much. Tears of pain, humiliation and rage rolled down my cheeks. Oh please, please God, I begged, I want this monster off of me and for the horror to end. It took a long, long time, but finally he was finished.

The pain was tremendous. I could feel so much fluid inside me – him, me, my blood. Blood. I thought I was going to die. I tried to get up to go to the bathroom, thinking it was over. Quick as a snake, Graham reached out, grabbed my hand and pulled me back down next to him.

"Did ya think it was over, sis?' asked my brother. "Hell no, we're just getting started!"

"Damn right!' added Graham who was again brandishing the knife. "I think it's time you started saying you're sorry to your big brother! Jack, boy, get over here!" Jack strode over to the bed, his erection bobbing before him. Without warning, the two men flipped me over on my stomach. Graham sat astride my back while I felt Jack get behind me between my legs.

Graham grabbed my hair and snapped my neck back until I thought it would break off of my shoulders.

"What's that you said, Jack?' Graham asked nastily, "You were going to give her an ass whuppin'? I think you meant your were going to whup her ass!"

Graham held the knife at my throat as I felt the tip of Jack's penis probe my buttocks…Oh God! No, no, no! This can't be happening! I babbled, I groveled, I begged, I prayed for him to not do it. Oh sweet Lord please no! Not that! Not there! Not my own brother!

White hot pain went searing through my bowels and I screamed louder and longer than I had ever before or since. My brother was violating me – and tearing me apart from inside. I closed my eyes as my breath came in short, squealing gasps with each thrust. Graham dropped the knife, wrapped his hands around my throat and started to squeeze.

"That's it, bitch. You love it!" Graham slobbered into my ear. With my eyes closed I started to get little black spots in my vision. Is this it? Am I dying? As if I was in another room listening to the assault, I could hear Jack's voice in the distance yelling, "C'mon, girl! Giddyap!"

Jack shoved Graham off of me, realizing that I had no more strength to fight, and pounded me harder and harder, shoving my face into the pillow until I almost blacked out from lack of air. Suddenly, he grabbed a handful of hair and lifted my head up and gave a gleeful howl with his final thrust.

I had been sodomized by my own brother. My life – it was nothing heaped on nothingness. I just lay there while the two men got dressed, laughing at me. Weakly rolling over onto my back, I looked down and saw my body covered in blood: cuts, scratches and a thousand welts and bruises."

Graham said he was going to get a drink and then do me again when I was something more than a "dead fish". Jack looked down at me and said darkly, "You heard the man, sis. It's time for you to 'soften up'. I have just the right tool for that." Brandishing his belt, the symphony of torture changed keys.

In the past, Jack had limited himself to hitting me on the back of my thighs or bottom; but that night all restraint was gone. He hit me against my back, my breasts, my crotch, my legs, each time leaving welt marks, while the metal belt buckle would tear out a piece of flesh. I tried to curl into a smaller and smaller circle, but he just continued to whip me. When Graham returned from getting his drink, Jack looked down at me in my ball.

"Oh shit, Graham," Jack said, "remember that fight with Little Tony? You picked him up just like that then threw him against the wall. And he bounced, right? Just went 'boing' off of the wall. That was too fucking funny."

"Yeah, I remember. So what? You think Grace will bounce too?" Graham replied.

"I don't know, seeing she's such a lightweight. But what the fuck, give it a try!" Jack snorted.

I heard what they were saying but I was past all understanding, even as I felt myself flying through the air and then crashing into a wall. I crumpled to the floor, a lump of flesh. Yet my tormenters weren't done. Graham thought I bounced while Jack said I just slid down the wall.

Graham laughed, picked me up and blindly threw me against the opposite wall – only instead of hitting the wall, he threw me against the large, plate glass window. The glass shattered on impact. My last conscious thought from that evening was "I can fly" – right before I landed, like a falling star, on the grassy area surrounding the reflecting pool.

When I regained consciousness a week later, I was told that I was still able to speak when the hotel staff came rushing out and fingered my attackers. Graham and Jack were taken to jail after the Tokyo police spoke to the hotel management. There was no doubt who had done this to me, as both of the men were splattered with my blood and still drunkenly laughing about my flying through the air.

As I recuperated for the next month in the hospital, I was able to get information from Goro, who had become my protector. He told me that the Tokyo jail is a terrible place for anyone, much less for two foreigners. Abigail came to Graham's rescue, with a large amount of money exchanging hands and promises that he would never return to Japan again.

Much later, I learned that Graham did not enjoy his freedom long. It wasn't much later that he decided to attack a whore back in the states in the same way as me – but her pimp had something to say about that. He didn't kill Graham, but let's just say that what he did do to him ensured that Graham had entré to any "members only" club in the world.

As for my brother, he remained in jail, for no one wanted to bail him out. About a year later, Jack was killed by an inmate. At the time, I was unsure of how I felt about that – to this day, I still feel the same uncertainty.

And me? I was a ruin of flesh and bone. Ironically enough, Jack had always promised he would never touch my face and it remained untouched. But the rest of me? Broken bones, hundreds of glass shards surgically removed, multiple lacerations, both deep and superficial. Goro, bless him, paid for it all and ensured that I had the best attention money could by. And when it was time to be released, he and his wife, Hana, insisted that I come to live with them – no arguments brooked.

I continued to recover in their beautiful home, surrounded by tranquil gardens and fountains. But as one bandage after another came off, so was ripped my peace: my body was a tracery of long, uneven scars. Some were short, but half an inch or more in width and filled with shiny, ugly red skin. Other scars were long, thin lines; but these were raised, looking and feeling as if there was an ugly, reddish, small rope stitched to my skin. But they all had the same effect: permanent disfigurement.

I asked the doctors, but they said that there was nothing they could do. They reminded me that I was lucky to be alive and whole. Yes, they were right: but still I felt as if my world had ended. I could never go out in public without people gawking at me if I left any of my skin uncovered. I avoided mirrors, hating to see what I now looked like. I, who had once been the Willows Girl, was now horribly scarred. I became more and more depressed.

Of all people, it was an old gardener who began to bring me out of my depression and give me a new direction and perspective. Once I was able to walk again, I would slowly stroll through Goro and Hana's gardens, where I would frequently see an elderly gentleman idly passing the time. I learned that he was their retired gardener, Nobu, and father of their current gardner, Yoshi. Both lived in a small house on the edge of their estate, where Nobu remained to enjoy his last years in comfort.

As I wandered through their gardens, I would often see Nobu gardening or sleeping in the sun. He would give me a look I was much used to – one that said, "You look familiar, but how do I know you?" Then one day, he greeted me with a big smile and motioned for me to stop. He held up a Japanese woman's magazine and, opening it to an earmarked page, grinned as he pointed to my photograph and then to me. As I didn't speak Japanese and he spoke no English, all I could do was grin in return and nod my head that yes, that was me. His obvious pleasure in having figured it out made me smile a real smile for the first time in nearly a month.

Over the next few weeks, we would often meet at a small gazebo and talk, with Yoshi, who spoke broken English, acting as translator. The old man seemed genuinely interested in life in America and how a single woman could end up so famous. I tried to explain that I really wasn't that famous, but he kept pointing to my picture in the magazine ad. The two men got over their awe of me, while I began to feel a bit more comfortable in my new damaged body. Although I still wore long skirts and long-sleeved shirts, I knew they could nonetheless still get a glimpse of the horrible scars on my legs, arms and torso.

One day, Yoshi and Nobu came to speak with me as I sat reading a book by a fountain. The son seemed almost embarrassed. I told him that there was nothing he needed to fear to tell me.

"I feel that my father is being impertinent,' said the young man, "but he insists on wanting to tell you this. So please forgive me and understand that my father is an old and very opinionated man who means no harm, he only wants to help you."

I was a bit confounded and, I admit, intrigued. How could a retired gardener help me? So I said that I appreciated his concern and was honored that he would want to help me.

"My father knows of your scars. We all do – although please understand that it is not as if we gossip about you; but still, you are a famous foreigner – very beautiful – then in that terrible incident – and now at our home. It is only normal that we are curious. Wait, wait! I am telling this all wrong. Again, it sounds as if we are a houseful of gossiping old women. Please excuse my poor useage of your language. Let me try again."

"My father has grown fond of you," said Yoshi, trying to compose himself and find the right words, "and admires you very much. Says you are a strong, courageous woman who should be living her life and not hiding out here. He knows that you hide your scars. He says that it is a tragedy to have even one mark on your beautiful skin; but it is more than just a few scars, correct?"

I said, "Yes, it is much more." Then, in front of these two kind men, I slowly raised the hem of my skirt and showed them my leg, covered with a spiderweb of interconnecting scars, the next uglier than the last. But then, after sharing this with them, I couldn't bear to see the look in their eyes. To my surprise, Nobu gently cupped my chin and lifted my head up to meet his eyes. With a glint in his eye, he made the universal sign of a curvaceous woman's leg and spoke to his son.

"'Again – please excuse my father. I know it isn't proper, but he insists I tell you this. He says yes, leg is marked, but it is still a beautiful woman's leg, curvy in all the right places. It is just the outside and that can be changed.'"

"Tell your father I appreciate his concern," I said, "and no, it can't be changed. I looked into plastic surgery; but since I am so badly scarred, they said that they might make it even worse. So, no change. All I can do is hide it so that no one is disgusted by it as I know I am.

As I told them this, I was on the verge of tears and wanted to run out of that gazebo and hide from all prying eyes. Nobu must have guessed of my urge to leave, for he reached over and gently took my hand in his. Then, looking at his son, the two men entered into a heated discussion. Back and forth they went, with the son finally shaking his head and turning to talk to me."

"Again, forgive me – or, rather, forgive the forthrightness of my father. I think you reach a certain age and can take liberties no one else may take. My father said don't hide. Yes, scars are ugly; but hiding them makes it worse. You need to make them beautiful, like you. Hide them in plain sight and turn them into something pretty."

No translator was needed for the two men to comprehend my confusion. I had no idea what he was talking about. Nobu spoke briefly to his son and then, letting go of my hand, began to stamp his foot on the flooring of the gazebo. The younger man then spoke to me.

"'I am so sorry, but we need to leave now as I have much still to do today. My father requests that you meet him here again tomorrow. And since I won't be here, he wants you to know that you need to look at the floor of the gazebo when you come back. He also suggests that you ask someone to tell you what happened to the gazebo a few years ago. Will you do that please?'"

I agreed and, more curious than ever, returned to the house. That night at dinner, it was just me and Hana, as Goro was attending a business dinner. Although her English was a bit shaky, we still managed to communicate. I asked her about the gazebo. The only thing she could think of was of an earthquake that had occurred a few years prior. According to Hana, there was a major one that hit Tokyo. Much, much damage everywhere. The gazebo survived the earthquake, but Hana understood that even that small structure had some damage. She wasn't sure where.

The next morning, I set off for the gazebo. Nobu was already there. From a distance, I could tell that somebody had given the small structure a thorough cleaning. It shone white and glistening in the morning sun. When I entered, I gasped when I saw the floor: it was embroidered with a beautiful, intricate picture of intertwining flowers that seemed to blossom from the very boards. As before, the old man stamped his foot. This time, I said one word – "jishin" – which is Japanese for earthquake. Grinning broadly, Nobu nodded his head and pointed to a corner.

I walked over, but did not understand what I was looking at or for. Nobu gently pushed me to my knees and squatted next to me. Taking my hand, he ran my finger over the stem of a flower painted on the floor. And then another stem. Back and forth I touched the two until I felt it: one stem was smooth on the floor, while the other felt rough with indentations. And yet just looking I couldn't see any difference because of the design and color. One was a crack painted to look like a stem; the other was simply paint. A marvelous illusion.

To be certain that I understood, the old man took my finger and traced the crack and pointed to a scar on my leg. In halting English he said, 'Tattoo make pretty.'

I slid from my kneeling position to sitting weakly. The thought was overwhelming. Could I be beautiful again? Was this possible? Nobu kept saying "Tattoo make pretty" while pointing from scar to flower, scar to stem.

I staggered to my feet and walked away. I didn't even think about insulting poor Nobu or scaring him into thinking that he had insulted me and that I would tell Goro and Hana. I ate dinner in silence – Goro and Hana were used to these moments and said nothing. That evening, while a full moon gazed down through the peach blossoms, I visited the gazebo. I spent all night running my hands over the painted images and then my scars. I could not find the crack. And neither would anyone else – ever again.

The next morning, I ran out to the garden where Yoshi was working on a flower bed with Nobu watching nervously. As I approached, they both leaped to there feet and began jabbering, Nobu in Japanese and Yoshi in half English. I raised my hands and made a "calm down" gesture. I explained to Yoshi to please tell his father that he was right – it was time to heal.

I spoke to Goro and Hana, who both nodded solemnly in agreement when I told them of my decision. Goro said that only the finest tattoo artist would do and that he would make an introduction – which happened the following day.

Suzuki Taro, the tattoo artist, examined my body. He spoke no English, so Goro had to translate. Suzuki said that I must completely trust him to answer the riddle of my scars. Trust. The word tasted like cardboard in my mouth. But, yes. It was time for all of my scars to finally heal. And so, I trusted.

It was Goro who struck upon the tattoos that mean the most to me – these one, here, on my arms.

"Grace," he said, "you are not the woman today you were when you first arrived here – then, you were the Willows Girl. Softness. Now, you are more. You are stronger. You are a warrior. Many would have died from your struggles, but you fought much – and fought off much. I say that on this arm, you draw an innocent girl to remind you of who you were and to never lose sight of your past. On this arm, a sword, to show the world the warrior that you have become and to serve as your standard for the future. You will always be both – let these be your eternal reminders."

I look out at the audience, raising the arms in the light so that they can never forget the sight. "These are the last tattoos you will see. Remember them. Know that the women in your life are no different than me – only that their scars are on the inside. They may cover the hurts that you give them with makeup or clothes and those will heal in time. It is the ones building up inside that you do not see that hurt the most. Pain drives the desperate to desperate acts. One night, I gave up being the woman on my left arm and the woman on my right plunged a knife into my tormenter. I was not the warrior I am today. He lived. Will any of you be so lucky?"

"Remember this lesson, this gift I give you – not because you are deserving, but because your women are – every woman is the Tattooed Lady. Pray you do not meet her – or me – ever again."

And then, the stage is empty.

No chair, no dressing table, no woman.

The men, who been hungering for sex, are starved for reason. They find themselves confused, gazing around the room at each other, questioning why they are there – not remembering why they are there – only that they need to leave, to go home to their wives, their families. To a man, they feel dirty, as if they had been thrown in a waller filled with the muck of secret shame and sin, filth that clogged their pores and gorged their mouths with putrid bile.

One by one, they stand unsteadily, staggering uneasily to the open flap of canvas that leads to the carnival outside. As they gain their balance and strength, walking turns to running – they flee for the comfort of the hearth, of the family.

Standing beside the tent, watching the stream of inhumanity vomiting forth, a man in a top hat idly fingers the skull on top of his cane. When the last patron vanishes into the darkness, the man walks into the tent, where on the stage coalesces a mist into the form of a woman.

"Do you think they learned something tonight?" she asks the man, now standing at the foot of the stage. The man nods. "I'd say you etched your lesson on them," he says and then adds with a soft chuckle, "You always leave a lasting impression, Grace." The woman allows herself a smile – he can always make her smile. "As long as I know someone can rest in peace tonight, I know that I am one step closer to being able to rest in peace forever. Until then, goodnight, Doctor."

As the woman returns to mist, the man respectfully, almost reverently, doffs his hat and deeply bows. Walking away, he dons his hat and says to the never empty night, "To have no yesterday, and no tomorrow, to forget time, to forgive life…to be at peace."

TENT 7

ENDS WITH "Y"
Michael Rennay

Dirt.

"Come on, shrimp – get up!"
"Aw, he can't fight – this ain't any fun!"
"Ah, nuts to you! Hit 'im again, Bobby!"

Looking up at the ring of faces staring down at him, it seemed that Jack was lying on his back at the bottom of a well. No use asking for a rope to help him up. The faces were angry. The mouths like open spigots poured down an unending deluge of taunts and jeers. But they were nothing compared to the fists that had dropped him into the depths.

He felt a pair of hands grab him by his shirt shoulders and lift him off of the ground.

"Look, shrimp," sneered Bobby Herman, "when we get back from spring recess, yer gonna gimme yer lunch and whatever money Mommy gives ya every day fer two weeks – if ya know what's good fer ya! That's yer payment for tryin' ta hit me back."

Giving him one last shake for good measure, Bobby threw Jack to the ground. Jack lay there with closed eyes, listening for the laughs and "That's tellin' 'im, Bobby!" to fade away in the distance before opening them again. When he thought it was safe to move, Jack's first action was to spit out the mud in his mouth, the mixture of blood and schoolyard earth.

Jack considered himself lucky. Only Bobby had beaten him. When he was on the ground, the others could have easily thrown kicks (as they had done in the past). Groaning, he slowly rose to a sitting position. He gingerly touched his face searching for new wounds – and he found them: a split lip, a bruise near his eye already starting to swell, a cut on his chin.

Even more slowly – and painfully and unsteadily – he got to his feet. Looking down at his torn and stained clothes he realized there was no way he could hide this most recent assault from his parents. Sighing, he collected his personal belongings that lay strewn about him and began the trek home.

"Oh, not again! Jonathan!" cried his mother seeing her battered son walk through the back door. His father came rushing into the kitchen and screeched to a halt when he saw Jack slumped in a chair. "It was that Bobby Herman again, wasn't it?!" he yelled. "Dorothy," he said angrily, kneeling next to his son to inspect his wounds, "Would you PLEASE let me do something about this?"

Jack started to shake, thinking that his father was angry with him. Tears welled up in his eyes. Jon Craigie immediately cradled his son in his arms. "No, Jack, no. I am NOT angry with you! I'm angry that this keeps happening to you." He pulled back and kept his hands on Jack's shoulders. He looked in his son's eyes with a reassuring smile and said, "Come on. You want me to clean you up?" Jack smiled back through his tears and nodded. "Okay," his father said, "let's go into the office."

Dr. Craigie was the town veterinarian. He always said, though, that he did as much to help out his human "pups" as he did the canine variety. Jack flinched with each daub of hydrogen peroxide, despite his father's always-delicate touch. "Well," said the elder Craigie, standing up with hands on hips to inspect his work, "That should do it. You're going to have a nice shiner, but those cuts should heal on their own."

Jack got up and went to look in the mirror. Yes, he thought, he was going to have these when he went back to school after spring recess. "Jack?" he heard his father ask. "Did you fight back like I showed you?" The elder Craigie, against his wife's wishes ("Violence only begets more violence."), had taught his son the rudiments of boxing, having dealt with the same height-related tormenting when he was a child.

"You held your fist up like this and then jabbed like this?" Dr. Craigie shadowboxed. Jack nodded. "But, Dad. That only worked against Bob- I mean, the kid who was in front of me. There was another one who shoved me in the back." His father rolled his eyes and grunted. Typical bully behavior: couldn't fight his own battles. He knew Bobby Herman's father, and the apple didn't fall far from the tree. The younger Herman was a pint-sized version of his equally abusive father, who also happened (unfortunately) to be the town's chief of police with a reputation for using (and abusing) his power with the help of his badge and cadre of sycophants.

"Well," said Dr. Craigie, "let's put all of this behind us, okay? It's your spring recess and I think we should start it off right. What do you say?" Jack nodded. "Well then," said Dr. Craigie, affecting a cowboy accent, "Time's a-wastin', pardner – let's go show your mother your fixed up kisser and go and find us some fun!"

The sun was losing its battle with the glow on the horizon. Jack watched that glow grow brighter as they approached it; and with the greater glow came louder sounds – he knew those sounds and his heart started to race with excitement. "Dad!" he exclaimed, "when did the carnival come to town?! None of the kids talked about it at school!" His father quickly turned around to talk and then went back to watching the road. "No one really knew they were coming, Jack. It was like they just kind of appeared out of nowhere." Staring ahead he continued. "I was over at Mr. Monahan's store to see if that new Lionel electric engine had come in yet when the wagons came through town. Funny to see horse-drawn carriages in 1947."

"Anyway, Mr. Monahan went outside and came back in with this," said Dr. Craigie, handing Jack a somewhat rumpled sheet of paper. Jack read, "'Dr. Sarcophagus and his Carnival of Dark Desires welcomes you to share yours with us.'"

"Jonathan!" scolded Jack's mother, "'Carnival of Dark Desires'? Surely you can't be serious about taking a ten-year-old boy to something with a name like that?!" Dr. Craigie responded with a soothing laugh, "Oh, come now, Dorothy. It's a gimmick. They're just trying to be mysterious and scary to draw in the adventure-seeking rubes." He reached out back with a free hand and scrubbed the top of his son's head, "I'm sure it's nothing our Jack can't handle!" Mrs. Craigie crossed her arms and grumbled out the passenger window, "Well, fine. YOU get out of bed and deal with him when he wakes up screaming from a nightmare."

Dr. Craigie just chuckled and shared a conspiratorial glance with Jack in the rear view mirror.

Mrs. Craigie's fears were at once realized and allayed shortly upon passing beneath the gaily-colored banner that marked the entrance to the carnival. Amidst the bustle of familiar faces of townspeople and the unfamiliar ones of the carnival dwellers, was the call of the barker to this tent or that, to this "spectacle beyond your belief" or that "person who will defy your trust in your own eyes." There were waferboards emblazoned with the lurid, suggestive images of such acts as "The Tattooed Lady" and disturbing, sure-to-be-nightmare-inducing depictions like "The Human Alligator." However, there were also shows with clowns, "little people," a fat lady and the like that she deemed tame – if not tasteful – enough to grudgingly give her assent to Dr. Craigie.

All thoughts of the day were dispelled, as Jack went amazed from one show to the next, with his father smiling to himself that his son's eyes would not return to a normal size for quite some time. Jack bobbed merrily on a sea of the unimagined and unbelievable – not to mention a powdery cloud of sugary funnel cake and rarely indulged soda pop – far from all cares, fears and concerns.

Towards the end of their stay, Jack was busily licking the sticky residue of cotton candy from the crooks of his fingers and deliciously unaware that he had fallen behind his parents. Until he heard, "Well, well, well – if it ain't the shrimp!" Jack froze. There was Bobby Herman with his parents. "Bobby!" scolded his mother, reaching down to grab his arm "That isn't nice! Why, you shouldn't –" Mrs. Herman was overruled by a burly, ridiculously hirsute man in a policeman's uniform. "Let him be, Lettie! Boys'll be boys! They gotta work these things out themselves." He put a meaty arm across her chest and pushed her back, leaving Bobby unfettered as his father continued to reprimand his mother for "interfering in being a man."

Bobby gave Jack an evil grin. "So, I guess it's just you an' me, huh shrimp?" Forgetting his cotton candy – and even his parents – Jack bolted into the crowd with a suddenness that momentarily surprised his foe and left him flatfooted. By the time Bobby gave chase, Jack had already melted into the crowd. However, Jack didn't realize his flight was without pursuit.

He ran, weaving in and out of happy, laughing patrons, often to a loud, "Hey!" or "Watch where you're running, kid!" Jack, thinking he still needed to hide, ducked down an alley formed between two tents that led away from the main carnival.

Looking back, expecting to see Bobby on his heels, he didn't see the man in front of him.

Jack bounced off what he thought was a brick wall. Lying dazed on the ground he found himself looking up at man standing directly over him. The man, dressed in a black and purple tuxedo and a top hat, was leaning on a heavy cane and gravely shaking his head.

"Young Master Jack," he said seriously, "we do NOT run through the Carnival, even when we think we have a good reason."

Jack was too frightened, both of Bobby and this new adversary, and equally exhausted from his marathon, to question the man's knowledge of his name. Instead, he blurted out, "But, mister! Bobby Herman is chasing me and he's gonna – "

The man cut him off. "'He' is going to do 'what', Master Jack? Who is going to do what to you?"

Exasperated, Jack pivoted on his butt, frantically pointed behind him and hissed, "Bobby Herman! He's right…there…" Jack was pointing down an empty, grass- and dirt-patched path.

Sighing, the man shook his head and said, "As you can see, we are quite alone. You seem to have the fleetness of Mercury, young Master, having left your adversary in a wake of dust." He extended an assisting hand and added, "So, unless you wish to – how do they say it – 'run away and join the circus,' might I suggest we help you find your parents?"

Reluctantly, Jack reached up and took the proffered hand. Judging by the man's wan appearance, he was prepared for a grip like a dead crappie. Instead, it was warm and firm, almost reassuring in its unexpected strength. Once on his feet, Jack began to brush himself off – his mother was going to kill him for the grass stains on yet another pair of pants. As he did so, he had the uncomfortable sensation that the man was, well, reading him – as if every inch of his skin was covered with words that only the man could see.

"Now," said the man, "Shall we look for your parents? Do you remember where you last saw them?" He started to walk back towards the carnival proper and Jack started to follow and speak – and stopped. He looked around and realized he was alone with a stranger, something his parents had always warned him against. The man sensed Jack's hesitancy and turned back towards him, giving him a reassuring, toothy smile. "Oh, I am so sorry – I have forgotten my manners," he said, doffing his hat and bowing. "Allow me to introduce myself: I am Dr. M.T. Sarcophagus."

Jack gasped. This was the owner of the carnival! "Yes," said Dr. Sarcophagus, reading his face, "The one and only. I know you were probably concerned that I was a dangerous stranger." He chuckled and threw a lanky arm familiarly around Jack's shoulders, "I am most certainly not the former. As for the latter, well..." He stopped and whipped his body down and around so that he was face to face with Jack – his eyes crossed and tongue wagging out of his mouth – and slobbered, "do YOU think I'm strange?!"

Jack burst out laughing. Dr. Sarcophagus straightened himself and resumed his earlier stately comportment. "Ah, the most beautiful music ever made – a child's laughter," he said. "I take it, Master Jack, that you have not been doing much of it as of late – am I correct?"

"No," Jack responded, suddenly at ease with this strange, but now familiar, man. As he spoke, his hand went self-consciously to his bruised eye. "Well, with my folks, yeah. But with, well..." Dr. Sarcophagus looked at him seriously and asked, "This Bobby Herman?"

"Master Jack, sit with me a moment," Dr. Sarcophagus said, folding his long legs down beneath him as he sat cross-legged, leaning against a sturdy canvas tent. Jack hesitated again; but something in the man's face and voice told him he should sit and talk with him. He sat down beside the carnival owner, who once again took off his hat and placed it on his lap.

"I will get right to the point and ask you a simple, yet difficult, question," Dr. Sarcophagus said. "Why has Bobby Herman singled you out to punish?" Jack hung his head. It was as if that question unstopped a bottle of hot, shaken soda pop and, instead of bubbly liquid, it was tears that burst forth. They sat for a few moments as Jack sobbed into his knees, which he had pulled up to his face. Dr. Sarcophagus did nothing to stop or comfort him, only giving him time to expend his grief.

When Jack was through, he looked up again through reddened eyes and saw a hand holding a handkerchief. He reflexively took it, wiped his eyes and face, and heartily blew his nose. "Now," said Dr. Sarcophagus, "can you answer my question?" Jack sniffed and, after a few dry, chest heaving sobs, angrily replied, "Yeah. He picks on me 'cause I'm the smallest kid in school and 'cause I'm smart and 'cause I can't fight back!"

"Hmm," Dr. Sarcophagus murmured, pursing his lips and resting his head back against the tent, gazing thoughtfully ahead into the distance, "that DOES sound like quite a conundrum."

After a few moments of uncomfortable silence, Dr. Sarcophagus stood up, put on his hat and said, "Well, now, Master Jack. This has been a most excellent diversion for me, and I thank you. Now, though, it's time to find your parents – they must be terrifically worried about you." Jack sat on the ground staring at the doctor in disbelief. He had expected some sort of profound statement about his situation, or life or something. Frustrated, he jumped to his feet and gave a muttered assent.

The two were walking in silence towards the growing noise of the carnival when the doctor stopped and pulled an ornate pocket watch out his vest. "Well," he said to no one in particular, "this is a bad state of affairs. Master Jack," he said, turning to the boy, "I'm afraid that I will have to leave you. I have left my carnival running on its own for too long – if I don't catch it, there is no knowing what places it might go."

"Don't worry," he continued, seeing the amazement on Jack's face, "Just keep walking straight ahead and you'll find your way. People who come to the carnival always do." With that and without another word or look back, Dr. Sarcophagus did an about face and disappeared down a tented lane.

Jack was alone. He should have been scared, but his anger buried the fear. First, the doctor reprimands him for running unattended through the carnival. Then he lets him roam similarly unattended. Fine, he grumbled in his head. Stupid carnival. Jack stormed forward as the doctor had told him, heading straight down the lane in hopes of finding his parents and not getting punished for his disappearance.

A tent.

Jack groaned. Now what? The doctor had told him to walk straight ahead, which led him to a dead end at a tent door. Paths stretched to the left and to the right, but he had no idea which direction was correct. This part of the carnival was like a maze. He looked back the way he had come, hoping to see his former host; but, like Bobby earlier, he was nowhere to be seen.

And then he heard the breathing.

It was loud. It sounded like a dragon was panting down his neck. He leaped a good few inches off the ground and spun in mid-air until he was once again facing the tent. Jack expected to see the tent flap billowing, but it remained motionless. Curiosity overcame fear and he hesitantly opened the flap and stuck his head inside. It was deathly still, aside from the sound of the breathing – and new sounds that were muffled to the outside ear by the heavy canvas: the gentle putt-putt-putt of a gas-powered engine and a rhythmic thumping.

In the dust-speckled, filtered light streaming in from an opening in the ceiling, he could see a large, oddly shaped metal box against the far wall – it was from there that the sound was coming. He slowly approached, looking around the tent: a cot, a few trunks, and a table filled with medicine bottles and all sorts of tools and things he had seen in his father's office. Next to the table was a folded banner with large lettering, obscured by the folds. Alone, but still aware that he was doing something wrong by trespassing, he tentatively unfurled the banner. "Talk With the Lady In the Iron Lung."

Jack dropped the banner like it was a hissing cobra. He looked at the box again – he knew what it was. And…was that…a head sticking out of one end? Jack simultaneously – and clumsily – turned and backed away. As he did, he caught his foot in the medicine table leg, knocking it to the ground and spilling its contents. Reflexes took over and he found himself sprinting out of the tent – until he heard the voice that stopped him.

"Please don't leave," it said pleadingly.

Jack closed his eyes, his back to the voice. Every nerve, muscle and bone wanted to flee. But there was something in the voice that held him fast.

Again it called to him. "Please come over and talk with me."

The heavy breaths punctuated the silence; but Jack swore that he could hear his own breathing over them. Swallowing hard, he turned to face the plaintive requests.

Yes, there it was. An iron lung. Mechanically, and almost against the rest of his body's will, his legs began walking him over. As he got closer, he saw the machine that he only knew from stories and the newsreels – terrible stories about people trapped inside prisons of life. He didn't know how they worked, only that for people with polio it was their salvation and their curse. His father had told him that the simplest way to understand them was that they breathed for those sick, paralyzed people who couldn't do it for themselves.

His palms started to sweat. Oh God, I'm standing here in a tent with a person with polio! I'm going to catch it and spend my life in a machine – I have to get out of here! He was still trying to make out the woman's face – it was obviously a female voice; but she read his before he could do the same. "Don't worry. You can't catch it – well, not by just sitting and talking with me."

Whoosh. Thump. Whoosh. Thump.

Something in the woman's voice comforted Jack enough for him to sidle in closer. Not just that: the more he looked at the machine the more fascinated he became with it. He thought it looked like a cross between a coffin and a submarine, with all sorts of wires and tubes going in and out of it. Even across the distance, the woman could sense his curiosity. "You can look at it more closely if you like – just don't touch anything."

Like a dog tentatively sniffing at a new treat, Jack crossed the cautious distance and began more closely examining the machine. There were small hammers that opened and closed rubber-sealed valves, and windows that, if the light had been better, would have allowed him to look inside. At the end of the machine was a giant version of the hammer and valve mechanism – this was what was making the heavy breathing sound. Transfixed, he watched it pump in and out; with each cycle emitting a sigh that sounded like when he listened to his lungs through his father's stethoscope.

Then it dawned on him: he and the woman had yet to be introduced. Jack felt slightly embarrassed about having ignored her to gawk at her metal lifeboat. He approached the top of the machine and gazed down on the smiling face of a woman who could have easily been his mother. "Hi there," she said, "It gets so lonely here. I'm used to having lots of people around; lately, though, well, they thought it best for me to be alone." She sighed and looked up at the opening in the ceiling. "Alone with the clouds." Turning her head to look at him she asked, "Have you ever flown?"

Jack disregarded the question. He was trying not to stare as the enormity of what he was seeing washed over him: a woman unable to walk or move. He thought she was like a prison inmate, only able to look out between the bars at a world she could see, but never walk upon. There was a mirror affixed on the machine so that she could observe what was going on behind her.

"I do that," she said with a sigh, going back to her upward gaze. "I can be anyone I choose just by imagining my story a little differently."

"In my story," she began, "I am princess trapped in a castle's highest tower. I was locked away because I had a power that frightened the king – he was afraid that I would use it to take away his people and kingdom. Each day is the same: I stare out of the small windows at the ocean over which the castle looks. I watch the seabirds gracefully skim the water's surface and run along the rocky beach playing tag with the incoming waves. I want to fly away – to leap from a window, spread my arms and soar in the sky like them.

"I thought you said you could fly," said Jack, shocked at the sound of his own voice cutting her off.

She smiled. "Every story is different – that is the beauty of it. Yesterday, I chose to fly – I did so the day before and the one before that. Today, I wanted a change."

Jack thought about that for a moment. He and his father would read (against his mother's wishes) a different comic book every night. What would it be like, he always wondered, to be able to live in the sea like Namor, be strong and smart like Batman or have Superman's x-ray vision? Without realizing it, Jack began thinking out loud. "Bobby wouldn't be able to beat me up if I were Captain America," he said softly.

"What's your name?" the woman asked, interrupting his reverie. Caught off guard, Jack responded, "Um, Jack." With his mother yelling at him in the back of his head about being rude, he found his politeness and asked, "What's yours?"

Again, she smiled. "My name is Shirley. Would you like to sit and talk? I could tell you more of my story."

Jack stammered, "Uh, well, thanks, but, um, my parents must be getting awful worried – I got separated from them and ran into Dr. Sarcophagus and –"

Shirley shook her head. "Ah, that explains it," she said, closing her eyes. Jack was confused. "Explains what?" he asked. "You're right, Jack," she said firmly. "I can see by the sky that it is getting late – you must find your parents before it gets dark. But can I ask a favor?"

Jack averted his eyes and kicked at the ground, "Er, what kind of favor?"

Shirley fixed her gaze on him. "Would you come back to visit me?"

Come back? Visit? No way! Jack thought. "Um, sure," he lied poorly.

Again, she smiled. "I have lived at the carnival for many years – long before I became, well…be that as it may, I can tell you the best way to get out AND back in." Jack wholly listened as she told him the former and only half-listened during the latter.

"Thank you, Jack. It's been nice having company. I – ah – ahcchh…"

Suddenly, her placid face contorted: her mouth opened letting out fluidic, guttural gasps and chokes; eyes grew wide and watery; skin turned bright red.

Jack's nerves, already on edge, snapped like brittle twigs. Suffering woman forgotten, he flew out of the tent, following her instructions on how to get back to the carnival's main avenue. Evidently, he was closer to "civilization" than he thought – before he knew it, he was back amidst the sensory bombardment of the carnival proper.

Above the noise he heard his father's voice. "Jack! Keep up – I don't want you getting lost. Do you want to be replaced with a kitten?" Up ahead, almost precisely where he had left them, were the Craigies – but how?! I'm going nuts, he thought. This isn't possible – I was gone at least two hours. Jack tried to work it out in his mind, but he was too exhausted to come up with any answers. Mrs. Craigie said to her husband, "Jon, will you look at him? He's like a wet dishrag hung out to dry!"

Jack's father got down on his haunches and looked at his son. "You okay, sport? I know: it's been a long day. You want to go home?" Instead of answering, Jack did something for the first time in his life.

And came to in his bed a few hours later.

Mrs. Craigie was standing over him, pressing a cold compress to his forehead. "...told that man the carnival was going to be too much for him."

As his eyes fluttered open and he became aware of his consciousness a horrible thought burst into his awakening brain and made him thrash so violently that he kicked his mother in the stomach. "I can move! I can move!" he started shouting. Mrs. Craigie was stunned by the blow; but quickly regaining her composure yelled for her husband. Dr. Craigie came bounding up the stairs yelling, "What?! What's wrong?!"

He found Jack jumping on his bed and running his hands all over his body. His wife was sitting on the floor, holding her stomach and soaked with water. "Jonathan Craigie!" she shouted, "The next time I tell you something I expect you to listen to me!"

Jack fell to the bed in a heap, crying. Dr. Craigie ran to his side and held him. "Jack, Jack – calm down. What's this all about?" Jack wanted to tell his father everything, but didn't think he would be believed. During his lapse of consciousness he had had a terrible vision of himself trapped inside a tight, metal box, unable to move. He was yelling to get someone to rescue him, but all he could hear in return was someone thumping on the lid and the sound of his own, labored breathing dully echoing against his prison. His fear turned to terror when, above the incessant thumping and breathing, he could hear Bobby Herman laughing.

How to tell his father what happened to him at the carnival, which he would naturally connect to his son's emotional state – he'd probably go to his old foe, Mr. Herman, and get him to close down the carnival. Why that bothered Jack so he couldn't understand – but something told him that was the last thing in the world that should happen.

"I – I just had a nightmare, Dad," Jack sniffled. Dr. Craigie responded, "I should hope to say you had more than that! Passing out? I wonder if that little bast- (Mrs. Craigie kicked Mr. Craigie in his dangling leg to cut off the expletive) Bobby didn't do more damage to you when he hit you. Stay here – I'll be right back."

As Dr. Craigie went to his office to collect some supplies, Mrs. Craigie climbed into bed with her son and started stroking his hair. "Are you SURE it was just a nightmare? You weren't scared by anything at that silly carnival, were you?"

"No, Mom. Really," Jack said, trying to sound convincing. She sat there by his side until Dr. Craigie returned. He checked Jack's eyes, reflexes and did some other tests. "Well," he huffed as he stood up, "He doesn't have a concussion – at least not that I can tell. I think, though, you should spend tomorrow around the house" – Jack started to protest – "ah, ah, ah," said Dr. Craigie, "That's doctor's AND Dad's orders – Mom's, too." Jack sullenly nodded and closed his eyes.

The following day was uneventful and Jack showed no lingering effects from the previous day's events.

At dinner that night, Jack started peppering his father with questions about polio, specifically iron lungs. As always, when conversations ran to topics that Mrs. Craigie thought were questionable for her son's consumption, she tried to change the subject. Dr. Craigie, of a more scientific bent, always felt that knowledge was the best weapon against fear. "Well," he said, trying to simplify it as much as possible, "people with polio become paralyzed and can't breath for themselves. So, the 'iron lung' as it's called pushes the air around the person's body so that it makes their chest go in and out so that their lungs work – do you understand?" Jack nodded.

"Can you catch it by talking to someone?" Dr. Craigie put down his knife and fork. "Jack," he said seriously, "I don't mind talking about this – but do you want to tell me why you're so interested?" Thinking fast, Jack answered, "I heard a kid in school talking about someone she knew getting it from someone else because he just talked with her. Another kid said that was baloney." Dr. Craigie chuckled and softened. "Well, 'the other kid' was right about the lunch meat," he said, pointing a newly engaged fork at Jack before plunging it into a piece of chicken. "You can't get it just from talking with someone. You get it from, um, touching their 'number one or two' or if you somehow get their spit inside you."

"JONATHAN!" Mrs. Craigie yelled, slamming her hands on the table. "Dorothy," Dr. Craigie quickly protested, "The boy asked! Besides, there's too much misinformation going around about that disease, what with so many people getting it and such. Better to be armed with understanding than ignorance!" Mrs. Craigie got up with a snort and began angrily clearing the table.

"Look, Jack," his father said, "it's a horrible disease and we have to understand that these are still people, no different than you or me. Remember that, Jack: different isn't good or bad – it's just different. And it's all of the different stories in the world that make it beautiful. I know it's hard to understand, but I know that a smart kid like you gets what I'm talking about."

"Every story is different – that is the beauty of it," Shirley had said.

That night, when Jack was certain his parents were asleep, he got out of bed, fully clothed, and clambered down the tree outside of his bedroom. He had never tried it before; but had always wondered if it was possible – Shirley imagined wings to take her away. He had an old oak.

Jack pumped his legs on his bicycle as fast as they would go. The carnival was out past the Lee farm, where he and his friends would go (without their parents' knowledge) in the fall to pilfer apples and in the summer to swipe strawberries. Once again, he was going there to do something he wasn't supposed to do – but this time, it felt right.

He parked his bike inside some bushes and walked the remaining hundred yards or so to the carnival's perimeter. The carnival was dark, aside from some lanterns burning here and there, illuminating random alleys and the cracks of a closed canvas window or door. Shirley had told him how the carnival was laid out and, despite his inattentiveness at the time, he remembered the mental map she had drafted for him.

Jack approached on the side directly opposite the main entrance. He shuddered to think that Shirley had told him that the most direct and least watched route also led beneath Dr. Sarcophagus' wagon. She said that he valued his privacy during a busy show week when he had so much to do, and that all of the family members, as she called them, respected his wishes.

He crawled, Army style, on his belly underneath the wagon, thankful that the weather had been dry. He heard no noise above him, nor had he seen a light coming from inside, and was grateful that the good doctor was asleep. Once past his primary obstacle, it was a quick jog to Shirley's tent.

A shadow of fear darkened his mind: what if she's dead? Jack thought. Oh my God. She could have choked to death and it would be my fault! Suddenly, the familiar sound of her life-giving machine made its way to his ears. Relieved by the sound and reassured by the glow from inside the door, he quietly poked his head in.

Shirley was there. From a distance, she looked like she was asleep. However, as he rustled the canvas with his entry, she turned her head and saw him. A wan smile softly lit up her face and she called to him. "Jack! I am so glad you came back. I knew you would." Her cheerful greeting made him feel ashamed of his behavior the last time, and Shirley saw his discomfort.

"Now, now, Jack," she said soothingly, "There is nothing to worry about – I'm fine, see?" and then she added with a sly grin, "Well, so to speak." Jack felt his entire body relax and this time approached Shirley without hesitation. He still felt he owed her an apology. "Shirley," he said, nervously clearing his throat, "I'm real sorry about how I acted the other day, and I – " Shirley shook her head, "Thank you, Jack – you're a good boy. But, like I said, no apologies needed." Brightening, she said, "I'd rather just talk."

Jack pulled up a chair, sat by her head and listened while she told him about her life, all of the things she did and saw. He heard about how Shirley's mother had joined the carnival after meeting her father. "I was – and still am – a child of the road. We are always moving – but we move together as one family on an endless journey. Every member contributes in any way they can, either in front of or behind the crowds. Dr. Sarcophagus always reminds us that each of us has a story to tell and something special to share."

She looked at Jack, almost peering through his eyes as open windows into his mind, "It takes some of us longer to learn what that is; but the doctor is very patient, like a…father. He doesn't tell us who we are – he helps us find out for ourselves. 'We all have a gift that only we can unwrap.'"

"I chose to be 'The Lady in the Iron Lung' to continue to contribute to the carnival. So, what some would see as a disadvantage, I turned into an advantage. Out there, people have forgotten that to be different is to be special." She hesitated. "Out – there, I would be locked away, useless…a…'freak'." She stopped herself and said, almost scolding herself – and Jack. "Understand, Jack, that we don't like that word here. Everyone here is called precisely what they are: special. And we are special because we are different. I know I must sound like I am talking in circles. But I think you know what I mean."

Jack nodded, swallowing hard. He was ashamed to use the word, even in his mind. Ashamed because he knew he had no right feeling sorry for himself and what made him – different – when Shirley was living proof that there was much more for which to be sorry.

The words came out before he knew they were leaving his lips. "I feel sorry for myself because I'm smaller than everyone else."

The statement burned him as it was uttered, as if he were spitting out boiling oil: Shirley didn't feel sorry for herself – and she didn't *ask* for anyone to feel sorry for her, he thought. She was proud of who she was because she saw herself as being important to the carnival – important to herself. "That's right, Jack," she said, again seeming to see into his thoughts, "This machine doesn't change who I am – just like being small doesn't change who you are. And it doesn't define who I am either. Always remember: it's *who* you *know* you are that is important, not *what* others *think* you are."

Shirley looked tired. Wordlessly, she faced the ceiling and closed her eyes. Jack sat there for a few minutes, waiting for her to speak again; but she had fallen asleep. He didn't feel the least bit tired – he felt good for the first time in as long as he could remember. He also had lost any fear of Shirley and put his face close to hers to make sure she was still breathing. Satisfied by the puffs of air being taken and exhaled, he quietly left the tent.

He found himself oddly comforted by the dark carnival lanes, as if the entire venture was wrapping him in a blanket and promising to keep him safe from the world. When he finally emerged from beneath Dr. Sarcophagus' tent and back into the world into which he had been born, he suddenly felt out of place – as if he belonged more, meant more, within the carnival than without.

As Jack pedaled for home, he remembered his first time at the carnival. He had laughed at, been fearful of and, in his mind, made fun of the acts. Jack braked hard and almost skidded off of the seat as the thundering realization hit him: he had been one of "them" – the people "out there". He clumsily one-leg hopped off of the bicycle, letting it clatter to the ground as he stumbled to sit there himself. He held his head and felt sick.

He was no better than Bobby Herman.

He sobbed, tears turning to mud as they mixed with the dirt. The fat lady. The midgets. All of them. They weren't "acts". They were *people*. They were *family* – *his* family. And he had behaved no better than Bobby and the other boys did when they jeered at and taunted him. Then Jack had another revelation. The people at the carnival all looked cheerful – like Shirley. Instead of resenting the audience, they embraced it: the carnival had its role to play and so did the customers. They could put themselves on display because it didn't matter what the audience thought of them – it mattered what they thought of themselves. And they *liked* themselves. They *liked* being with their family and doing what was necessary to keep the family fed and clothed. "Always remember," Shirley had said, "it's *who* you *know* you are that is important, not *what* others *think* you are."

The next morning came at nearly noon.

Jack got up, washed, dressed and went downstairs ready for breakfast. His mother was outside gardening and his father's car was gone. He glanced at the clock – it read 11:30 am. Jack had no idea what time he had finally gotten back in and into bed; but it must have been awfully late (or early) for him to have slept so much. He poked his head out the back door and its creaking alerted his mother to his presence. "Well, well, well! If it isn't His Highness!" she said sarcastically. "Did your Lordship have a good rest?"

"Aw, Mom…" Jack demurred.

"If they haven't turned into record albums, there are pancakes in the covered pan on the stove," she said, before turning back to her azaleas. "Mom? Can I ask you a question?" Jack asked. His mother stopped pruning, put her hands on her knees and replied, "Sure." Before he could ask, Mrs. Craigie's brow furrowed. "It isn't something about what you and your father were talking about the other night, is it?"

"No, no," Jack quickly answered. "I was wondering…what did you think about that carnival?" Mrs. Craigie rolled her eyes. "Oh, don't tell me you want to go back! I don't care what your father thinks: that really is no place for a child!"

Jack pushed. "Why?"

Mrs. Craigie angrily took off her gloves and slapped them to the grass. "Why? Because children shouldn't be exposed to those kinds of people, that's why. It isn't healthy." She caught her breath and calmed herself. "Jack. I'm not saying they are *all* bad – they just aren't, well, like normal people – like us. They're…*different*. Does that help?"

"Thanks, Mom," Jack lied, "it sure does."

Shirley looked pale; but she still gave Jack the same beaming smile he had come to expect.

"Hi Jack! So, what did you do today?" she asked brightly. Jack was too embarrassed to tell her about his conversation with his mother, so he told her how he had spent the day lying under a tree re-reading comic books, thinking about what she said about writing his own story.

Shirley nodded. "Well, that is a good way to start – to see how others imagine things. But I can help you a bit more. Let's play a game – do you feel like it?" Jack was always up for any kind of a game and said yes. "Good," said Shirley. "Here's how it goes. I'm going to start telling a story. I'm having a bit of a time breathing lately, so I'm going to take a break and let you keep it going. Then I'll pick it up once I'm rested. Ready to give it a go?"

Jack was unsure; but he could tell it would make Shirley happy so he agreed.

Shirley began.

"I'm back in my room in the castle. The king still has me locked away, afraid that my special power could turn the people against his evil rule. I spend every day alone with no one to talk to except the birds. The person who delivers my food was chosen for the job because he is deaf so that he (I know it's a he because I see his hands) can't hear my voice."

"One day, a curious page (that's a boy who works in the castle) is wandering the halls. He sees a mouse running along the floor and decides to try and catch it. The mouse scurries under a tapestry and the page pulls it aside thinking he has it trapped – instead, he finds a long, dark staircase. The page – let's call him Jacques – doesn't have many friends. He wants to catch the mouse so that it will be his friend."

"Jack – could you continue? I guess I'm more tired than I thought," she said, winded.

Jack started to sweat. He never liked being called on in school, even though he almost always knew the answer. This was different – it was one thing to know the answer to, "What is the capital of Nebraska?" and something entirely different to be asked to continue someone else's story. He was afraid he would sound stupid and embarrass himself.

Shirley, sensing his nervousness, said, "Don't worry, Jack. This isn't a test. Just say whatever comes into your mind." Jack took a deep breath. "The page wants the mouse, so he goes up the stairs. It's really dark and he's scared. But he really wants the mouse." Jack was trying hard to tell the story the way he thought Shirley would tell it. "He climbed for a long time until he bumped his nose on something hard and fell on his butt." Shirley snickered – it made Jack feel good to make her laugh.

"Someone was inside the door – it was a woman. She heard the noise and asks, 'Is someone out there?' Jacques answers, 'Yes.' And the woman asks, 'Who are you?' And Jacques answers, 'I'm Jacques. I'm a page. Who are you?'

"I'm a princess trapped in the tower," the woman replies. "The king locked me away and I have no one to talk to. Will you talk with me?" Jacques is scared. The king? He didn't want to do anything to get in trouble with the king – he chopped off the head of a page younger than Jacques for knocking a flagon of wine on his shoes! "Uh, I think I should be going," Jacques says hastily. The voice from inside is pleading. "Please stay. I've been alone for so long – just for a little while."

Jacques is torn. He knows what it is like to feel alone; but he also worries how alone his body will feel without a head. It only takes a few moments for him to decide there is no harm in talking with the woman for a while – after all, how often does a page get to talk with a princess? "Your highness?" he asks, "I'll stay and talk if you like."

"Oh!" exclaims the voice from behind the door, "Yes! I would like that very much!"

Coughing. Wheezing. Jack's reverie was broken. Shirley was having trouble breathing. Instead of running away, he leaped to her head. "Shirley! Are you okay!" The woman made a choking, gargling sound. Jack put his hands under her pillow and lifted up her head, which helped her to clear her airway. She gave watery blinks and shook her head – her mouth looked full to bursting. He put her head back down and she craned her neck to the side and spat out mucous-laden fluid that formed a vile pool, soaking her sheet and pillow.

Jack froze. "You get it from, um, touching their 'number one or two' or if you somehow get their spit inside you," his father had said. But he couldn't leave Shirley lying like that. He looked around and saw a pile of clean, fresh towels on a chair next to the medicine table. He remembered a gangster movie where the detective had to save a woman from a burning car. The metal was so hot that he couldn't touch the handle, so he wrapped his jacket around his hand. Jack wrapped a towel around each hand and clumsily picked up another. While Shirley watched with a mix of relief and admiration, Jack sopped up the mess and, getting another clean towel, wiped her face and neck. He then took another towel and positioned it so that she was lying on a clean, dry cloth.

As soon as he was done, he carefully unraveled the towels, making sure not to get any of Shirley's spit on him. He had done all of this in silence – and it was Shirley who broke it.

"Thank you, Jack," she whispered hoarsely. "You and – a person – here at the carnival are the only two who have helped me like that. The others…" Shirley closed her eyes. It looked to Jack like she was fighting back tears. "I don't blame them," she said, her voice cracking, "I wouldn't want to be here either." She began to cry in earnest. "Well, Shirley," Jack offered, saying the only thing of which he could think, "you don't have to be here – if you feel like it, can we keep telling the story."

"Jack," Shirley said through her tears, a smile working its way like the sun through the clouds of a passing shower, "everyone can be a hero, even if they aren't Captain America. A person does what he can – but a hero does what he must." She sniffed back her tears. "Yes, that's right," she said, Jack thought, to herself. It seemed to calm her. After a few moments, she said, "Okay, Jack. Let's get back to the story. Do you remember where we were?" Her voice was breathier and softer than it had been. Jack nodded. "Yes, Jacques had decided to stay and talk with the princess. Are you sure you're okay?"

"Yes, yes," replied Shirley reassuringly, "I'll be fine. Once we finish the story, I'll get some rest."

"So," she continued…

"Jacques, being an honest, straightforward boy, asked the princess, 'Why did the king lock you in there?'"

Jacques heard a forlorn sigh. "Well, the king is not a nice man, and – " Jacques interrupted her. "Your highness! You mustn't say such things!" He stopped himself in mid-scold realizing that he had just shushed a princess! "Your highness! I am so sorry! I didn't mean to – " It was the princess' turn to interrupt. "Have no fear, Jacques. I am not like the king. I like it when people speak their minds." She added with another sigh, "In fact, that is why I am here."

"What do you mean?" Jack asked.

"As I was saying, the king is not a nice man and no one likes him. There are the few people with whom he surrounds himself who claim to be loyal – but they are only so because they are afraid of what he will do to them."

"The king thinks he is strong – but that is because no one can get close enough to challenge him. And that is what he fears. He knows that he is weak and that without his so-called friends and guards one could knock off his crown as easily as you could sweep dust off of a table."

"You have been close to the king, haven't you?" she asked? Jack replied, "Well, yes. I once had to deliver a letter to him."

"And did you think him terribly big or strong?"

Jack thought about the question for a moment. "No, not really. I was kind of surprised that he was smaller than I thought."

"There you go!" the princess said triumphantly. "Why, even you, Jacques, could tweak his nose if you wanted!" Jack couldn't stop from giggling at the thought. "And there are many people who would like to do just that. The king locked me in here because he knows that words have power – and that I know how to wield that power to make others free themselves from their fear."

Jacques was intrigued. "How, your highness?" He heard the princess laugh. "Why, I have already shown you! Have you not overcome your fear of being punished for talking with me? Have I not made you realize that the king is no great giant to be feared? And didn't I make you laugh – because you know you could do it – at the thought of tweaking the royal beak?"

"You see, Jacques," the princess said with a sound of conclusion in her voice, "If people truly believe they can do whatever it is that they want to do, then they can. Of course, I don't mean that you can go and grab the king by his nose; but you have the confidence – and strength – to recognize what is right and wrong and take a stand for or against it."

It all made sense to Jacques. He thought of all that he feared – and all of the people he feared – and realized that he spent so much time being scared that he didn't bother to look for the alternative. To be strong. "Princess," he said, his voice full of conviction, "I believe you! I don't want to be afraid anymore! How do we get you out of there so that you can help the people learn, too?"

The princess answered, "Jacques – open the door." Jacques reached for the latch. It did not matter that he hadn't the key, or that the door was too heavy or that he could be punished. All that mattered was that the door stood between him and the princess – and nothing would stand in his way.

The door opened upon a sun-bathed room, filled with the ocean breeze and the sound of seabirds cawing over the surf. The princess was lying on a bed facing a large window. She turned her head to Jacques and smiled. "Thank you, Jacques. You have set me free by setting yourself free. You have given me strength by finding yours. You are the words now – all you have to do is just be you, and you will be me."

The princess returned her gaze to the window. She heaved a great sigh, her smile more radiant than ever, and closed her eyes.

"Jack."

The unfamiliar voice brought him out of his reverie. He shook his head as if coming out of a dream. What an amazing game – it was better than reading his comic books! "Shirley!" he exclaimed, leaping to his feet. "Can we do that ag–"

Jack froze.

Shirley's eyes were closed. Her skin was pale, with an almost bluish tinge. But on her face was the smile he had seen so many times – and the same he had seen on the princess. And then he heard it.

Silence.

"Noooo!!!" he howled. "No! Shirley! No! No! No!" A pair of strong arms wrapped themselves around him and held him fast. "Jack, lad. There is nothing you can do," said a voice behind him. Jack writhed and kicked, cried and screamed, wildly flailing against his captor. The arms were too strong – and too comforting. Soon, his anguished energy exhausted, Jack went limp.

As he felt himself being picked up, he looked at Shirley and then turned to look at the face of the person in whose arms he rested.

It was Dr. Sarcophagus.

He carried Jack to a cot and laid him down. He pulled up a chair and sat down beside the bed. Jack looked up at him and uttered one, weak word: "Why?" Dr. Sarcophagus shook his head. "Master Jack, I have lived longer than you can imagine. In all of that time, that is a question for which I have yet to find an acceptable answer. And would you like to know why?" Jack nodded. "Because there is no acceptable answer."

Jack was tired. He couldn't think. He shook his head in impotent frustration. "I'm sorry. I wish I could offer you more – I honestly do," Dr. Sarcophagus said with genuine sadness. "Why should a good woman die? And why should she perish in such an ignominious, undignified manner? We could easily ask, 'Why does the disease exist that afflicted her?' or 'Why did she have to be so afflicted?' Again, Master Jack, I have no answer. For my part, I don't believe we are entitled to one – nor do I think, if we could have it, would we want it."

Jack sat up in bed and looked at Dr. Sarcophagus. The man did not seem to have the same swaggering aura as he had when they first met. In fact, he looked more exhausted than Jack felt – his arms crossed at his knees, hands clenched together and head slightly bowed. Standing up, Jack walked to the side of the tent where Shirley rested – finally. She did, indeed, look peaceful, thought Jack.

How long had he known her? A few days? And yet in that time, he had learned that she was a good woman – and had learned much from her. "It was good to have her in your life, wasn't it, Master Jack?" asked Dr. Sarcophagus. Jack turned – the doctor hadn't moved; but, for not the first time, it felt like he had read Jack's thoughts. "Yes," Jack answered. "It was – I only wish – "

"That you had more time?" finished Dr. Sarcophagus. "Yes, I know. But aren't you better for having had her in your life, even if it was for just a short time, rather than having never had her there at all?"

Jack started to cry. He reached down and brushed her hair with his hand – it was the first time he had ever touched her. So much fear, he thought. But she had – or the princess had – shown him that being afraid gets in the way of things you ought or need to do. Jack leaned down and kissed her forehead.

"Goodbye, princess," he said as he wept, "And thank you for your words – and strength."

With a last kiss, he turned and strode back to Dr. Sarcophagus and, wiping away his tears, confidently pronounced, "I am coming with you."

Dr. Sarcophagus did not move as he spoke. "So, the scared, young boy who was so anxious to find his parents is now willing to leave them to, as I said, 'run off and join the circus'? Are you so certain that this is where you will find the answer to 'Why?' – or to the rest of your questions?"

Jack said resolutely, "I just know that I belong here – not 'out there' – because I'm 'different'. And no one 'out there' likes different people – not even my mom." Dr. Sarcophagus slowly lifted his head to look at Jack – and Jack felt fear looking in the man's eyes. They smoldered. But if he was angry, the doctor's even voice hid that anger. "Is that what you learned from Shirley? How to run away and hide from your fears? Did I not just overhear you thank her for the legacy of her strength?" Dr. Sarcophagus stood up, crossed the room and looked down at Jack, who felt himself growing smaller by degrees. "Always remember, Master Jack, that it is up to you to define who you are – not others."

Dr. Sarcophagus walked over to Shirley. He reverently placed his hands on her iron lung and bowed his head in silence. The church-like stillness was broken when the doctor said solemnly, "My daughter has given you a gift – and an opportunity." He slowly turned to address Jack directly. "Yes, you may, indeed, be 'different' – but not enough to belong here." He paused. "Not yet, at least."

Jack opened his mouth, but was cut off before he could speak.

"Master Jack," Dr. Sarcophagus said, striding over, "you can serve a greater purpose 'out there' by standing up for yourself – and others – who are different. By teaching others – like your mother – that different people," Dr. Sarcophagus said, placing his hands on Jack's shoulders and leaning his face down to look him in the eye, "people like us, are special. And that without us, the world would be a much less magical – and more boring – place."

They stood like that for a moment that seemed to last forever. And in that time, with their gazes fixed on each other, Jack looked deeply into Dr. Sarcophagus' eyes and saw nothing but his own reflection.

And smiled.

The next day, the wagons of the Carnival of Dark Desires clattered back through town, past Mr. Monahan's store and out into the world from whence it had come. Jack Craigie was not there to see it leave, just as he had not been there to see it arrive. He was sitting at the desk in his room, staring out of the window at a tree – a tree that grew close enough to the house to let him clamber down its length a boy and climb back up a young man. Jack pulled a few, fresh sheets of paper out of his desk and with a sharpened pencil began to write.

"There once lived a princess who was locked in the highest tower of a grand castle for being different…"

This way to the exit...

On behalf of our family, I want to offer everyone my sincerest thanks for attending. I dearly hope that you were entertained and edified, and are looking forward to returning – soon.

Why do I qualify your return with a sense of urgency? Because like a darkened landscape illuminated by a flash of lightning, what you see here may be gone when the storm abates and the dawn comes: we are in danger of disappearing in a flood of public outrage and social indifference.

As we enter a new "modern" era filled with scientific miracles, I fear that my show may not be around – or welcome – much longer. There are forces at work in government and public opinion that label such as we as frauds, scoundrels and, in some circles, devils. But, as you now well know, that is not what we are.

Don't you?
Excellent.

However, I can assure you with confidence that it is up to you: we will always be here if you do the following. Attend and offer up your precious pennies when you see the wagons rolling by your home. Come to us when the siren smells of popcorn and funnel cakes permeate the air. Follow that all-too-human need to be entertained when you hear the cacophonous music from our aged calliope singing in your ears.

Finally, and most importantly, come see us when your darkest desires need fulfillment.

Until we meet again (and I assure you, we will), I remain

Very truly yours,

Dr. M. T. Sarcophagus

Dr. M.T. Sarcophagus

ABOUT THE RINGMASTERS

Mitchell Hyman is a comic book industry veteran whose work has been recognized and endorsed by such respected industry personalities as George Perez, *Green Lantern* creator Mart Nodell and *The Flash* creator Harry Lampert.

Mr. Hyman created the acclaimed independent character and eponymous comic book *Bubba the Redneck Werewolf*, which received solid reviews from diverse print and online publications, including *The Chicago Tribune*, *Wizard* magazine and aintitcool.com. He also gained notoriety for his work on *Cracked* magazine, in particular the Donald Trump firing issue.

Dr. Sarcophagus and his Carnival of Dark Desires is Mr. Hyman's second book, following *Hitmen in Paradise* published by Double Scorpio. *Hitmen* was the first installment in a projected series of books revolving around two guns for hire, Vinnie and Mook, who find themselves entangled in supernatural events, which they try to deal with using their "conventional" methods.

Jeffrey Stundel has worked as a professional marketing writer and editor for over twenty years in a diverse spectrum of industries, including financial services, publishing, Internet, education and the performing arts. His work has appeared in all media – print, web and broadcast – for such notable firms as Merrill Lynch and in publications ranging from *Time* and special *Newsweek* supplements, to local New Jersey newspapers, including *The Princeton Packet*, *US1* and *The Times* of Trenton. He currently serves as the president and creative director for Boheme Opera NJ, a not-for-profit arts organization in central New Jersey.

Richard C. Livingston's talents have graced movies, television and video games. While working for animation powerhouse Nelvana, he worked on such television shows as *DROIDS* for Lucasfilm, *Babar* and *The Smurfs*. Invited to join Walt Disney Animation, he served as a layout artist on, among others, the feature films *Mulan*, *Tarzan*, and *Lilo and Stich*.

Following his tenure at Disney, Mr. Livingston went on to design spacecraft for the *Battlestar Galactica* and *Caprica* television shows, as well as *The Bionic Woman* and *Virtuality*. Currently, he works for computer game company n-Space, having worked on such titles as *Marvel: Ultimate Alliance 2*, *Star Wars Battlefront: Elite Squadron* and the military franchise *Call of Duty: Modern Warfare: Mobilized*. Most recently, Mr. Livingston has done design work for *Terra Nova* and created Santa Claus' high-tech S1 sleigh for Aardman Animation and Sony Picture's *Arthur Christmas*. www.richardclivingston.com.